THE OBSERVATORY

Also by John Fraser
and published by
AESOP Modern Fiction:

Animal Tales
The Answer
Behaving Well
Best Friends
Black Masks
Blue Light / Starting Over
The Case
Confessions
Down from the Stars
The Ends of the Earth
Enterprising Women
The Future's Coming Everywhere
Happy Always
Hard Places
An Illusion of Sun
The Magnificent Wurlitzer
Medusa
Military Roads
The Other Shore
People You Will Never Meet
The Red Bird
The Red Tank
Runners
'S'
Short Lives
Sisters
Soft Landing
The Storm
Strangers and Refugees
Thinking Scientifically
Thirty Years
Three Beauties
Tomorrow the Victory
Wayfaring

THE OBSERVATORY

JOHN FRASER

AESOP Modern
Oxford

AESOP Modern
An imprint of AESOP Publications
Martin Noble Editorial / AESOP
28a Abberbury Road, Oxford OX4 4ES, UK
www.aesopbooks.com

First edition published by AESOP Publications

A catalogue record of this book is available from the British Library.

First edition 2009, revised 2014, 2020, 2024

ISBN: 978-0-9561409-1-3

CONTENTS

ONE 7

TWO 55

THREE 165

‘Are they willing to lose all the comforts and charms of our existence, to have barbarian youth rather than civilized senility, untilled soil and virgin forests instead of exhausted fields and artificial parkland? Will they demolish their ancestral castle for the sole pleasure of helping lay the foundations of a new house which will be built, no doubt, long after our day?’

A. Herzen,
From the Other Shore.
Year lvii of the Republic.

ONE

SOMEONE HAD LEFT a tumbler of gin on the bedroom floor, and its insistent smell woke him up. He could see in red neon across the street 'Fly to Isfahan – for roses and nightingales.' Some stray burghers were hammering on the railings which had closed the mouth of the underground. Three policemen going off duty let their conversation float upwards:

'I only ever beat up one old man – for pleasure that is.'

'One must give and take a few blows in the new social war: even a dying empire must suppress its neo-proletarian element.'

'What do you mean, exactly?'

Their voices wandered away down the cold night streets.

He groped over for the gin. It smelt of tall blue porcelain. It made a cool infrangible column as he drank it. The leaping figures in the panopticon stopped their capering as the gin called for order and boldness.

'Negate my negation' said a handwritten sign on the wall – the end of some festive game, he now saw, had filled his room with merry thoughts. 'For a General Strike of Generals', 'Lions, be sure your foxes are Earthed.'

It had not been a good party: but if he became drunk again,

he could postpone his hangover – perhaps indefinitely. The distorted gibber of a century and a half of empire swashed and gurgled like ethereal waves. He pulled the notices down.

He thought of yesterday's drinking: swanning through the Strand's bars like an unruffled old queen – 'Recessional' he would call it. A cheesy row of faces, men rearing up against the rampart of the counter, studying themselves for ever in the mirror behind the whiskies – the companionship of the bottle waited to be scourged to death. Then he had lunch in the 'City of Nets' – the table pitched like a roof tossing wine out of the glass and food off the plate. Finally, a drink at twilight in a pub snug as a sitting room, full of gay metropolitans in vicuna suits – beautiful unsmudged loungers with vivid laughs. He had admired the splendid girl who served him – her contempt for him surging freely from a millennial vindictiveness. She treated the other customers gently and with humour, but for him she had the face of the ancien régime, forced to keep open house for conscript revolutionaries.

At his party, he had been forced to listen to a friend urging him, for his own good, to give up a girl who had in fact refused to see him for months. He felt himself shrinking. A friend said, 'We opened our old Christmas pudding – the one reputed to have been sent by Marx: but it couldn't have been more than thirty years old, at the most.'

'I hear they have an attested specimen in Amsterdam.'

'That's most unlikely.'

'He's very witty and he sells dogs.'

'We don't *need* to smash the unions now – and we've such a technological start ....'

'Sure it fell down, but we'd sold it by then.'

Somewhere in Montenegro hay was being sledded out to grateful sheep: in England, though it was midway to dawn, trucks still bothered the late and early hares. If only he could find someone who could touch him – not for nostalgic reasons, to cure an illness, or to reawaken their own youth. But someone new, to whom his opinions staled by so much swashing around in his head seemed affronting and delightful. Those washers and jetons from the dark – perhaps these were really sovereigns? Would some young girl, fresh and exultant from her struggles with the Lincolnshire squirearchy, love him for his verbal coinage, as one loves the man in the next cell who taps 'Comrade' on the wall? Much more likely his evening (or morning) would be taken up with considering when to change from beer to doubles, and whether he had been asleep at the bar.

'All Englishmen are tired,' said the inscription over the staff college gateway – or was it a motto on the wall of that imperial banting-house where the tired servants of the queen went to sweat off their colonial surplus?

'Having lost the empire,' said another policeman, 'can't we have a bit of leave?' The gin was over now – but here was the girl!

'I'm so sorry, Curzon, I've been locked out, and I've no coat. This policeman wants to go home – can I sleep here?' Arching his nose for more gin, Curzon left his sea-swollen bed and unslept dreams, setting out for a brisk five hours on the run in London.

'Yes, naturally: do sleep here. It's no trouble.'

He sat for a while on the stone step of the pub Tom Mann

had kept: a jungular mist was rolling in from the suburbs, and at times obscured notices to visiting Americans telling them how to elect their president.

'Got no work?' asked a street cleaner.

'If I had, I'd not be doing it yet. It's only five o'clock.'

'I've crossed the river twice this morning already. Some people always win—'

'I'm a teacher anyway, so whoever loses, I win.'

'I've always wanted to teach.'

'Perhaps you will, one day.'

'I doubt it.'

'I wouldn't know how to start cleaning a street.'

The other's whimsy turned easily back to contempt. 'Better move then, squire: the rubbish you're perched on belongs to my council.'

Suddenly, he was riding a midden – no, in fact just a heap of whitish earth. It was rushing backwards, pressing him clumsily against a wired wall. A hard edge of moon came in sight, occluded in the lower horn by a small photograph of Ravachol. A long way away someone was shouting, 'Get on out of there … Get the hell out of there!'

His stomach went dead and he thought: 'I think I must be going to be nothing.' If he stayed quiet, he would soon outpace the man who was shouting – no doubt that had been a Chagall refugee, prowling in urban lanes after lovers and chickens. Bump bump went Curzon's body as it thrashed about on the earth bank. In his head was a crude gyroscope, undoubtedly manipulated from outside, which looked like two large dice. Even as he watched, the Ravachol face flipped over, and on the fresh face, he counted eight spots; eight sides? No, for the next face was blank, and he had forgotten to allow for Ravachol. The next blow of the dice turned him hazardously on to his back.

'Get him out of my garden.'

But there really was no one there. The next throw of the dice produced a brochure. 'The only way to approach is from the North. Or you might try, as we did, the over-ice route from October to May.'

'If only I could get back to Ravachol.'

'Here, this bloke'll take him. Careful now, don't spill him.'

The taxi left him in his flat. Someone had broken in to leave there some broken chairs and a firestick. He tried to find some coins for the firestick, but the door had been bolted on the inside, and if he were not careful he would be unable to find his way back. The bed seemed very full of other people. A guslar began to sing softly outside. Only Curzon slept untroubled as the governments of friendly and unfriendly states began to unload new groups of citizens at the abattoirs, or to intern them.

When he woke up, the girl – Elizabeth, wasn't it – she said: 'I sent the police away. They wanted to know about the chairs. This used to be a proconsular suite, you know.'

'Let's go to Isfahan when I'm well again. Roses. Nightingales. Whatever can a firestick be? I was convinced I had one in here. How odd to get so ill when there's no need – I've to be in Tienen today.'

He considered how every journey requires a theory of aesthetics, how every journey should constitute a dislocation of conventional perceptions of historical continuity … Could mere travel revive his flat, his two-dimensional fortunes? Sliding – half drunk – from continent to century, until some concern caught at him, stopped his slither—

‘We’ll follow our noses across Europe—’

‘And in Tienen, what?’

‘If you come, Elizabeth? I know you so slightly, I don’t think we’d be unhappy, out of very terror. Let’s pack some sets of dice, to play for drinks. Tiny monarchical worlds of hazard – offering false chances where only the tequila is not random but darts to the gut like a tiger. In Tienen we will perhaps find a tedious man, an acquaintance: he is to give a lecture tomorrow.’

‘?’

‘Imagine the written part of Marx – the plans not only of a universal city, but the plans for an architecture, a drastically restructured personality to inhabit this projected civilisation, plans in fact of present and future. Marx himself doing some building and from these efforts extrapolating more plans – even building on the basis of meticulously scaled and detailed plans themselves derived from the general plan. In Belgium we can start looking for this general plan – it may be Marx’s, or another’s or indeed a plan of a kind no one has seen before. We shall be moving with one foot in sociocultural time, and one in sociocultural space. You’ll soon learn to hobble along the like the rest of us. We won’t be sticking to one century or one social system. People will glide in and out – pacemakers, laggards – indeed, poets and peasants, peasant poets, poets exploiting their peasants and peasants conscripted to gun down their poets. I promise you that the fantasy will be the fantasy of the real world, and that however much the people jigger about like parboiled ninnies, they'll be cast-iron real.'

'I think you're looking for a universal theory of misery and disappointment. I certainly shan't come.'

He wanted her to come with him.

One does not mind writing in only two dimensions, and watching these flat concepts sidling about from page to page and flowing on to the tablecloth. Perhaps conjurers are adventurers in the fourth dimension, their tricks the everyday life of the booming well-rounded fourth-dimensional bullies who plod and trample around us. But by acting in the few dimensions we have, we override the limitations of our own two-dimensional scribbles. He hoped that, just as the problem of the firestick was subsiding, the problem of Elizabeth might grow to overshadow his isolation – and, who knows, on the top branch a (probably mechanical) nightingale?

'I want you to come with me. Why not be the problem to overshadow my isolation? Don't you fancy an adventure in the dialectic? Let me at least run through a reel or two: I won't spoil the ending – and do feel free to improvise!'

'I am deeply drawn to your mind: I even like the silence it makes when it is not working.'

'That seems very coy, though, I suppose, flattering. Watch you don't become just a figment of what you admire. When we go off to the mountains to synthesise our concept once more, you may find you've been dematerialised.'

Curzon believed so deeply himself in the value of mental interconnections and was accordingly so ineffective in managing the physical and factual ones – especially with girls like this – that he found it easy to expand his consciousness without the attrition or erosion involved with other people.

They arrived in Tienen after some pleasant enough arguments over the hospitality offered by some gothic old sports in the ship's bar. Rolling the dice for rounds of Chartreuse, timing the waves with their stopwatches, the sports had been a breath of old England straight from the gated roads of the stone-blind midlands.

Curzon thought that he would obtain useful proprietorial skills by steering Elizabeth round the system factors and brokers of the West – ingratiating himself in a manner not wholly amatory, but still the interesting side of busybodying. Calculated practice – with the child's self-mazing self-conceit – and self-deceit – so that perhaps he *would* let himself fall for real. At the Iron Gates, possibly, hearing them clank shut as he and Elizabeth scuttled deeper into the warm heart of socialism.

'What I like about Belgium is that the Whitbread frontier stretches nearly into Germany. I owe Whitbread's more enthusiasm and patriotism than any other British institution – except possibly Worthington.'

'These people in the bar were sweet. One cried when you told him a sailor had been snapped in half by a hawser as we sailed.'

'Muddied oaf. That was a lie. He'd already said he could have beaten their strike, so I threw that in to make him ashamed. No credit to him, it made him maudlin. I was only concerned lest a small error I made should have swamped the boat. The washroom had a saltwater tap which I turned on and couldn't extinguish. It seemed we were lower in the water when we docked.'

There were several phalanxes of fascists in the square at Tienen. They wore carnival heads or fibre helmets, painted to resemble iron, to avoid recognition by the police. Chattering through the chubby heads of baby-bland festive politicians, through the long snouts of cool-eyed carnivores, to their comrades-in-arms, the iron-headed crocus-shoots, they seemed to welcome the violence their absurdity encouraged. The police practised the slash and the lunge with their long truncheons, happy enough to have heads of a new consistency to pound away at on an afternoon of political excitement.

'Ours is the other group,' said Curzon, 'the party of the angels. Over there – on the other side of the dialectic.' He pointed to it – a cable for the television crews. Elizabeth realised that he must have divided his time on the boat between her and the tourist bar, and the first class bar upstairs.

Softly, sweetly, gently, they strolled through the kite-strings of troupes of children in smocks. Street musicians with pottery tambours, dyudyuks and dragon-headed lutes, scrambled among the kites and the cables, sneering and spitting. 'Shades of the charnel house,' said Curzon, noticing the slivers of goose and turkey membranes used to pluck and patch the instruments.

Far over the fields flew a scarlet balloon, carrying the president of an association of anarchist – or at least *anarchisant* – civil servants. They could see him waving and hugely laughing as he neared the town, but local warm air wafted him away – racked with glee, nearly tumbling from the gondola. Elizabeth and Curzon joined their procession – a genius of sublation had allotted banners each with a single word – which read sensible from front, or rear, of the procession – but which was its own walking, singing, chanting negation.

'Red or black, it's all the same to me,' said a woman in front of them. 'They'll none of them stop the cows giving milk.'

She said this with such satisfaction that Curzon asked, 'What's all the same?' but Elizabeth hurried him along. At the head of the procession a motorcycle policeman was weeping, but he put on his goggles and outstared the stare.

In Brussels a television producer gave the word to his crew, and the processions began. Curzon galloped forward with his advance guard towards the fascists, but mobile police separated them. 'Why did I do that?' wondered Curzon.

Under the tall candles of sticky scented trees, the children played with their kites. The balloon rolled back and nestled down among them. The popular front procession was in full flight, gloomily negating itself as the bearers turned tail, gradually shedding concepts and sense, as the longer words were thrown away to assist the retreat, and the shorter words prodded into police and nationalists.

'Quick, into the gondola!'

'Christ, he's gone mad,' thought Elizabeth, who did not put all she saw into as many sets of words and synonyms as Curzon, and had in any case not noticed that the balloon, snared by a fish kite, had drifted into the square.

As they rose above Tienen, they could see fighting in the streets. The television cameras burst like glass furnaces. The friendly fringe of suburban streets was filling with men from artisan tenements, the fires of the factories had been scattered over the shop floors. Harrows were dragged over the mosaic floors of the town hall. 'We shall win because we are the stronger' floated up to them, but they could not tell from which side. The first heavy camions and the hard black noses of tanks were ploughing through the fields towards Tienen.

'Since we are clearly not to have the chance of hearing my friend talk on the future of future, or whatever, I shall have to deliver the address myself,' said Curzon.

'Quick, then,' said the anarchist. 'Believe me, I'd not miss this for green smoke. But those kids in the square sew razor blades in the kites' tails to rip what they may. I thought if I laughed they'd reel their machines in – but they didn't. Red as little foxes, I hope?' he asked them.

The collapse and destruction of social harmony in Tienen, which had as its first victim some sociologists on fieldwork, martyrs to the trade, carried on below them. Feathers of burnt paper quivered up towards them.

'I have been trying these many years,' Curzon began, 'these many necks of these many woods, to run my time backwards. Living a clean and decent faustian life, but in my mind unravelling time as you ravel it. Let's put it another way: ideas are simple. Let's have a war, thinks the general manicuring his big proud horse, that should give the workers something to think about. But he doesn't need to have the idea of Lancer Mroszek sitting in a field full of fever and sloughed limbs eating rye bead in the tenth year of hostilities.

'If only we could have ideas as involved and fantastic as real conditions, we fantasists would have to carry less criticism. No one says that it is absurd to have had the First World War – or that it is absurd to think that another war will break out. Yet if our idea of the First World War covers what happened to some real – or imaginary – people or places or things for four years, or our idea of the next war includes a projected index of Austrian industrial production, one is accounted a fool. Why is this?'

The President thought rapidly as they drifted towards the ground in some country, 'Why do they put anarchists in prison? To confirm their faith? How pleasant if every state decided it did not want its anarchists, and would give them an island, pineapples at the heart of every bush, a lemur hooked on every branch, where they could renounce he rewards of citizen obligations and discover whether they were an historical moment or a society out of time.

'In my last prison, there were no rats. So we used to feed the warders, call them pet names, be sad when they went away or died. You could say in fact that we socialised them. Angry at first, they let themselves come to depend on our largesse – we could not love each other, so we loved them. Up to a point. The point where we were let out. No one wants to walk back into the world with a pocketful of prison rats.

'Unlucky Tienen. Sad to see two groups who are deprived, fighting each other. However incongruous an alliance between them, better inconsistency of this kind than to shout to the first tank from Brussels, "Liberate me!" and receive the 80 mm shell in your throat.

'I feel like an early barbarian showing later folk-waves the best places to loot, those women who are not rather jaded by the whole business of conquest, saying, "Of course, don't make too much mess. We've all got to live here, and it is more comfortable if you leave the roofs on the buildings and the grain in the granaries. And please don't throw anything unpleasant in the wells."

'But of course, off they strut, to poison all the water. It is satisfactory enough to see them lying about a week later, faces shrunken and sneaky like mink and fox in their shrouds. But by that time one is alongside them oneself. If I could only construct a Bokhara of the mind – a militia waving gladioli, peasants in green hats carrying scarecrows in national costume out to the fields. Wooden walls to keep out the wolves, naturally, and some teams of camels to help out with the road work. Tall birds among the reeds, cows in the rice fields, half submerged in deep summer. Mausolea full of dried grass and pinks – the rose mosque bursting through with foliage at the top, like a neglected onion. And I shall live there, and no one will talk to me, nor I to them, since I shall have invented for this city a language which only I understand. I need only leave there when I'm hungry or cold.

'And then someone else will have to fuss round me and do what I tell them.'

'We are still living in the folds of your literary outer garments,' said Elizabeth.

'Listen to what this man has to say,' said Curzon, as they recovered from the shock of the casual destruction of Tienen.

'I drove a truck in the Soviet Union for two years. Up the mountain and down the mountain ten times a day. Little fox faces hoping for twenty hungry miles that I'd miss a corner. In the evenings, cards, drink, talking of the sweet future with our faces the faces of the damned. One of us came from Kronstadt – and he used to have nightmares of the troops coming towards him across the ice in their white parkas, great squares of rotten ice cracking and rearing, short, calling shells throwing spouts of yellow and grey water into the air. He'd such a torment from the double aspect of things that he used to sit all night on a huge rock, awaiting who knows what comeuppance.

'There was a man too who had been in the defence of Madrid – a Mexican – who had left his post out of fear, or boredom or whatever. It had seemed so easy, he said, just to walk away: and there were in any case so many people anxious to take over his machine gun that he did not consider that he was giving up what he later referred to as "his historic role".

'"How can I get it back," he would ask, "when I've missed it all?"

'And I would tell him the role he played was historic all right – he had just helped along the losing of a war – and that was history.'

Try again, thought Curzon. Fasten the memories together and you invent a new causal chain. Invent a new memory and you gain something on the unknown. Try another drink, another country … and yet this is all wrong.

Playing endlessly by the stream in Silesia, waiting for the field grey or the white parkas, depending on the season and the direction of the wind: crying 'Momma, is that the fire brigade?' As they come with hoses that can pour fire, and momma is skeetering up the road thinking, 'They'll get him, anyway.'

Even the squirrels, who expect to avoid this sort of thing and even to keep a few caches of nuts through the campaign, realise that it is better to pull out. Loading the drunks into police wagons in Boston of a weekend – now, instead, the broken pieces are in Tienen.

*

There was a general strike on when they arrived. ‘We are heroes,’ said the posters the doctors carried. ‘We too,’ said the banner the fish cannery workers bore in procession through a thicket of giant lilies. ‘Break down the barriers which divide one organisation from another,’ said a leaflet, ‘no Peruvian socialism here. Let all produce: let the self-activating workshop exalt the proletariat … invent new machines and you gain something on the kingdom of the unknown. An end to the administration of things – we are wares who would act as men: defeat us and we stay defeated. We allow ourselves no second chance: defeated, we will join you in reformism, chess, coffee and bagatelle. End our heroism and you will have only your native tedium to share with us.’

‘How can we help?’ asked Curzon.

‘On the contrary,’ said the railwayman, ‘we must help you. Since we are making history, an act of magnanimity here or there is not without intrinsic value nor political meaning.’

… and try again – build the structures before you can begin to exist …

Pepper under the Cossacks’ hooves, the clandestine paper slipped into *Time* or *Newsweek* and sent through space (if only sociocultural space), prisoners wearing themselves away like cicadas to pen political testaments in their own fluids – suns or rotational phenomena? With what devotion to change other people, other things – and to change oneself. No stranger, perhaps, than Berlioz, cursing the coachmen and innkeepers of Europe, wondering in what key he should send Faust to hell. Curzon remembered after a performance the radio announcer had said with a coy chuckle, 'The damnation of Faust took rather longer than we expected.'

Under the plane trees, only the click of beads: some monks nearby were cutting up parsley, deeply covering a long table. In this, the old capital, partisans had riddled some tired old icons with machine gun bullets: the palace was carved to resemble a cottage loaf under lace. In the church, priests had carved 'I am a good priest', 'I am worthy of heaven'. 'Is heaven worthy of me?' – even 'I too could have been a bishop' – relics of the days of general illiteracy.

Along the goose-meadow Curzon and another Elizabeth had gone, chirruping back to old Moldavians whittling, or cleaning sparking plugs.

'Tell me now,' she had said. 'Now or for ever never.'

She is going to spoil all this, thought Curzon.

'What, if anything, do you feel about me?'

So it has come then: of course, the miserable tension and the certain knowledge that the shaft of space beneath one is not curved, no feather-bedding on the bottom. How much courage, though, to say one would like to run away!'

Why ask *me*? he thought. Ask the apricot trees or the cranes.

'I don't know that I want to be bound by my own prediction,' he said.

'Right, that's enough then.'

'But of course you know how much I *feel* about you, don't

want this to end, etc.'

'I know now precisely.'

'Best to leave it there in future?' mused Curzon: he had always thought it bad form to make any declaration less than one of undying love to most of the women he met. They seemed excited by the prospect, and as long as one had frequent rests and had a flexible range of emotional response, it was usually possible to outlast one's partner. One's honesty of manner could usually rescue one from the lies one's words attempted to convey.

In the waterfront tenements they work a twelve-shift week, which meant the legal imposition of a 180 hour legal maximum, which is usually reduced by the employment of child apprentices, and by irregularity of work. In practice, once the tourists start arriving no more work is done till January of the next year. The visitors are delighted, if scornful, to see everyone idle when they arrive.

The federal constitution works like a dream, and when the Prez family dies out, will be visible in its ideational glory. In the heart of every bush there lurks a pineapple. A visiting bishop was amused that an orphan described the year of his religion as 'At Christmas you get the biggest piece of meat you ever saw, and when He dies you get a bun.' Last autumn a lot of people were killed by the police and put in a quarry: the local doctors claim that a disease which they call '*Aufhebung*' (and laugh) has wiped out most of the secondary school graduates in the last few years. The sole legal function of most of the city's parties is to sell shirts, and those parties are accordingly classified as 'archaic' or 'prehistoric', and everyone waits for them, somewhat impatiently, to catch up with everyone else.

In the new blocks of flats …

No, thought Curzon, it is still all wrong – we're not running fast enough …

My girl, my girl, don't lie to me, where did you sleep last night? In the village the song played out to the cows from the loudspeakers, and with a hop and a hiss from the tape switched on to 'Vingt Ans', and then the 'Sea Interludes'. A man in sheepskins was watching a hole in a snow bank, hoping a rat would come out. A few miles up the road a company of pioneers in white parkas was lashing logs together for the first tanks of the winter campaign.

The teleprinter limped out 'Tienen is burning' to the party headquarters of Europe. In a graveyard by the sea an elderly painter grubbed about for bones to grind down for the paintings which were, he hoped, going to burn down his own neck of the woods.

(More literature, said Curzon to himself):

Hear us
O
Higher elephant

said the poster that the fig-merchant held between his toes.

In Austria Curzon was able to work for some time on the papers of Otto Bauer – not the Austro-Marxist. but a painter and social philosopher who wryly had produced a cosmology which was to produce a red Vienna in a few years. The librarian sneered at Curzon's strange lack of German – the more odd as Curzon had taken the trouble to learn Flemish, on the grounds that Belgian strikes were more interesting than German ones. The only thing that would persuade him to learn German, Curzon always said, was the proof that German had been a minority language in the Habsburg Empire in the last century.

Bauer was a man whose head was stuffed with all kinds of nonsense: he'd clearly never heard of Walras, was still thick as thieves with Lombroso, and had once been introduced to Sorel's mistress in an ice cream shop in Deauville. Nonetheless, he had contrived to transcend all this, and retain his humane and voluntarist outlook. He had been a friend of Schiele, and his last crumble of bones in the Alto Adige had been identified by a letter from his friend. His last statement, before committed to his reluctant sacrifice of all that mattered to him, or indeed anyone, was impressive.

'If the bastards kill me, they will do so without my permission or acquiescence. When cooperative workshops cover the world, when lianas cover the gas works, when the children in schools no longer remind me of people drowning, then I shall know my sacrifice has been doubly in vain. I shall have been sent to my death by people I despise, and the world produced by an infinity of pointless deaths will be one I should love to have seen. I shall not excuse my death, and shall be very angry with people who suggest that after all it did not matter. Little did you know, you survivors, what I'd in mind to say …' And so on.

Curzon much enjoyed what he could understand of the papers, and drank enormously in the evenings under the suspicious eye of the librarian. Curzon believed that a litre was about half a pint, and so went to bed early every night swinging on strawberries, tulip beds, red and pink cardinals cartwheeling like electric gladioli, and woke too late even for hangover. The librarian hoped that Curzon would find that Bauer had been a proto-fascist, and though he had, with the ignorance especially reserved for librarians, never looked in the folders of Bauer's letters, he was made angry by the gay laughter which Curzon produced of a snowy afternoon. The library itself was hidden inside a colossal statue of Hilferding which had been laid out in the 1930s, but never hoisted upright, so the library was lit by skylights not windows, and instead of stretching over a fountain like the Italian archive, Hilferding sprawled with a catalogue in his forearm, reading rooms across his chest, and temporary doors cut in floor and ceiling.

The only upright statue in the town was of Francis Joseph feeding the birds: the local anarchists were so disturbed by the form avian gratitude used inevitably to take, that they protected the emperor with a tarpaulin, so that only one bronze arm poked out from the dung-covered cape.

They found Austria abrasive – but the fantasy bubbled high in Curzon's mind …

The library staff used to come in at the weekends to burn archives for which they had no further room. Curzon and Elizabeth would search through the rubbish, saving diaries of the seven weeks' war, dolls made by prisoners, photographs of the executions of Bosnians. Once they found a sequence of designs for vestments produced by someone at the court of Stephen the Great – princes in their gardens, tiger lilies and pointed trees, tin fences to keep the wolves out – and in the distance a boat – triple-steepled like a church – with a wolf-face poking out.

Tormented, Curzon continued his fight against necessity, against himself, and against his class – against all classes, retreating always with the selfish and self-indulgent courage of the solitary …

'Who is this woman?' Curzon wondered. Bauer, whose papers had after all proved too insubstantial – as well as eventually too sardonic and elliptical – to sustain a book, had said: 'The further east you go, the more you slip from one administrative dimension to another, creeping from one page of the ledger to the next, or burrowing through the spine, the greater the difference between the companion you see and the same companion who sees you. For the east (which for us in Vienna must be always fantasy and troubled dream) which lies in your imagination will one day be penetrated by the real thing. Only men with imaginations of the most superficial kind could wish to visit other worlds – since here there are an infinite number of onion skins to be peeled away. But to travel on the earth is to stretch your imagination to the limit – and ultimately means you must either submit to fantasy or die of it – or at least break through not to accept fantasy but to dominate it and yourself create fantastic things.'

And as usual, Curzon could not be quite sure whether Bauer had written a life of Curzon, by a kind of morphological prevision, whether he was a metaphysician, or whether what sounded like sweeping fancy was really a hard and ruthless awareness, however elliptical.

The works of Bauer had been pursued throughout the

institutional body of Hilferding – Curzon himself had searched a hand and an arm while Elizabeth followed up capillaries picked out by the catalogue. In the inn the vine was sour, and still Curzon could not decide whether he loved Elizabeth or his artifice, and could not understand why she allowed him so long to make up his mind. It seemed, indeed, as if this allowance of time was in direct proportion to the finality of any decision he eventually made.

At night they could see the bonfires of archives the librarians made: Elizabeth, who had plundered the smouldering heaps for mementoes at the start, seemed now to be relieved to see so much of the human baggage-train being destroyed. But the ashes silted up the rivers and covered the snow with soot: for weeks the clouds over the valley were pink with flame and yellow-brown with smoke. Curzon sat rolling dice, right hand against left, staring out of the window like a goldfish staring at the wall of its bowl, wondering whether the wall was transparent and distorting, or whether the world was after all just one other puzzled goldfish, pivoting on its nose the better to observe the ellipse of its body trailing behind.

At times they drank together, Curzon and Elizabeth, feeling the interior shell peeling away from the outside, achieving some kind of communication because they shared vertigo. The little yellow chariots of wine nudged them gently down the long green slope to that internal alp where innocence and ignorance, unconsciousness and false consciousness lay down together in the same alcove of the thesaurus.

'I'm afraid I objectify you so much,' said Curzon, 'that I know everything you think, and why. It doesn't spring from communion with your inner mystery, I'm afraid – it's just determinism. I think you're probably someone I'll always love – but why should you bother? I don't suppose we'll be happy together – because you're part of my cultural baggage. It's a long hot journey to come – I want to lighten the load. This would be absurdly priggish if I wasn't sure that you'd soon get irritated with my stubbornness. To offer to release you, however harshly I do it, is the least selfish thing I can do, given that even to please you I cannot lessen my discontent and my abstraction.'

'You would need to work on it – just to become a camp-follower is too easy,' said Elizabeth sadly. 'When he so wants activity, why should I assume that he prefers death to love – can't he simply long for action?' she asked herself. But she knew too that whatever the answer was, she could not faithfully give it – since, after all, her love demanded that he should have no choice in preference to her love, whether of action or death. Common sense said much the same, and Curzon himself did not invoke the dialectic.

'Bauer died up there.'

With a thousand other skullbones riven simultaneously, no one to hear the last quip – at that moment Bauer himself surely feeling it really hardly mattered if anyone did or not. Probably another internationalist killed him. That would teach him to ignore the forces of atavism on his next appearance among us, thought Curzon sourly. The centipede squashed on the wall like a question mark – or is it an exclamation mark – is usually a miniature of one's own end.

There are in fact only two kinds of violent death – interrogatory and exclamatory – and Bauer, like most of us, chose to go out with the big question unasked. But then, for me, he answered it ten times a day. Who needs answers when there are vineyards? The big theoretical question of the hour for me, thought Curzon, is whether socialism can be built in the presence of Elizabeth. And since by asking the question I know it cannot, I have to decide on what scale I wish my failure to be: slide off with her and never see the sun of socialism dawn or away with her and see myself slide off my theoretical basis into petty-bourgeois evolutionism.

Curzon thought: in the great search for innocence corrupted – that is, a corruption which preserved its innocence, or ignorance – how distressing to see the young burdened with their fathers' ideas and prejudices, like military greatcoats. Like the entombed of Verdun who could stand motionless in their bronze paint for hours, the contemporaries of Bauer used, to his irritation, to respect tradition in a society where traditionalists hated them. Intellectuals exaggeratedly respected the wishes of those who would burn out the intellect with the brands they used on their pigs or horses.

'Today I saw a worker spit on the red flag,' wrote Bauer, 'and I felt pity for his misery, anger at the party's propaganda, and misery that this man's need for a total transformation of the conditions of living should prevent him from taking the first necessary step towards the pinprick of light at the bottom of the eggshell. Only people who have a lot can sneer at another man's hope – and only people who are despicable can kill his hope.

'Let every man who has a fox set it to steal grapes; let every man who has a lynx set it to knock off the unattended wine jar. Let old men chirruping in the sun – "We have come through" – reflect that though there are giant tortoises with '1789' carved in their shells nuzzling through the bushes (a pineapple in the heart of each one), it rained most days in their youth. Why did their cargo never come, never the prince's ransom wash up on their shore – only the cigarettes tossed from the tank hatches, chewing gum from the civil administration, while the children warped with rickets like chair legs on a lathe and auntie went blind mad in the cowshed through the hot summer of 1911?'

The colours of the proletariat are red and grey. ('We must go south,' said Curzon.)

In the forecourt of the mosque the storks hopped professorially among maize. Painted sheep snored: sticky-sweet from the lime trees scented the leaf-flicker and the hot fretwork of the branches. Pigeons pecked among the bones in the graveyard. In tiny forges boys of nine and ten refurbished the rusty skeleton of dead capitalist cities. You could ride in De Sotos and bootleggers' Buicks. An itchy Byzantine sickness stole up from the clean sea, irritating the beggars' stumps.

This city was wearing out – sections broke up and crumbled into the sea, or were shipped further into the interior, where the cavalry practised the defeats of 1917 till it had them off perfectly. In the next country there were cities where you had to hop two feet down from the pavements on to the unmade road bed. Old steel erectors playing tablars in lunch breaks felt quite pleased to imagine the completed concourse which would link the opera house with the folk museum in which they would soon have a place.

In a bar in Bosnia an American was saying to his companion, 'Look, I know all about Europe: I helped pull their fat out the fire fifty years back. Take this place, Sarry – Sahr – Sarajevski – a bit of private enterprise is all they need.'

The owner of the bar smiled. The Americans thought without rancour of returning to their public corporations which lived on contracts for boots for the government's army which was fighting the allies of Bosnia in Asia.

(and East)

'Six thousand political prisoners built this,' said the guide proudly. In a clump of cinnamon trees there were statues of the gods in various positions – realising, playing imaginary instruments, releasing doves, sitting in the "inturned' position and so on. Their pointed hats poked up above the topmost leaves. Monkeys raced about with heather in their paws. A bus called 'Hang on, we are the sickle' fumbled among its gears before starting its penitent's crawl up the hill outside the village. A policeman stopped tormenting a Trotskyist peasant leader and went off to relieve himself. A man selling evil eye charms read 'The most beautiful pages of Otto Bauer'.

'Do you drink in order not to feel fond of me? Or in order not to have to think about me?'

'I drink because I feel fond of you and don't want to think about my feelings. The answer to all feelings is "It can never be" or "But it just isn't like that." Why should one want people to have similar feelings to one's own about them, when one really wants their behaviour to fall into a desired pattern? I don't care what your feelings about me are, because I've no wish to know, as long as I drink enough for our behaviour to coincide. You remember the question, "Which is more beautiful, the blackbird's song before it sings, or just after it has sung?" While it's singing, it is just a scruffy old bird hopping up and down, whistling away the time between one worm and the next.

'So let it be with us, and why should I worry if you say what a slouch, what a timid fool? If the essence of the game is to secure coincidence of feelings – there are mine: I don't expect you to be so foolish as to entertain similar ones, and you can imagine how tedious it would be if indeed we both felt like this.

'So, as long as you don't turn this into a system of power we'll just stand together like two chairs at the same table – close, even identical, but sat upon by different people.'

The innkeeper brought them two more jars of honey.

It was a night of great tiredness: the guard of the agricultural penal colony spat down a hundred feet into the grey water where big fish slapped their tails and golloped flies. Police boats flickered off the shore with naphtha plangent across the waves. In the background were lamp standards to be erected, mountains to be climbed. The cicadas had stopped scrubbing away at themselves and had turned back into leaves.

Curzon and Elizabeth kissed, each thinking of someone else.

You've no right to burden everyone else with your lassitude, thought Curzon. But one can distinguish here function (at which I'm deficient) and personality. Darling Elizabeth, as one might say, darling chair, so comfortable to sit down in. Darling everyone, how nice not to know you all.'

It was at Argos that the third world war had broken out that day, when Curzon had mistranslated a headline. 'A good place to die,' Elizabeth had said laughingly.

But Curzon had very much not wanted to fall out in that café, turning himself inside out with the force of his cathexis, to see the proprietor – keen to translate menus into forgotten languages – burnt up like a locust on his own battery of ovens. Even the man across the street whose deficiency sores had spread all over would have run from the new quip of God's providence, had it come spitting lava like golden fleece indeed, down the street.

Curzon had run in to see the hotel porter, with his paper conscientiously pronouncing sentence of misery. The porter said, 'I was in the army during your war, and then during our war. I promise you, next time, I wish to be a victim, not a participant. When I saw my comrades killed, and myself killed them, I thought that I must know who next I killed. It's easy enough to be killed. It's knowing enough to make it worthwhile for them to kill you that matters: and if you know that much, you must also know that it is pointless to kill you.'

'Weeell,' said Curzon, ready enough to start an argument in extremis.

Elizabeth wondered only when the bitterness of this drag around Europe would end. Who was to marry here and demonstrate the new dimension? Eh? And yet, she really did think like this, when the fishes' tails rang out like gunshots across the bay, and to be the last person to leave the soft integrated evening was more important than anything.

Swept here by the dying tide, Curzon watched the files of orphans wandering through the foxgloves to look at the sea.

Nuns sailed through the sand, over-masted, slipping their blue and white canvasses into the wave tops. One of them kicked fiercely at a little boy who had fallen over. They stood between the children and the rude ungodly sea. A few hundred yards down the beach were submarine sheds.

Bauer had wandered here, towards that mixture of lunapark and rotting potato tenements, the heart of red Vienna. The roads seemed to have been laid over rubble. A white horse was dying with a crowd around it.

(I see: I drink: I write: I think. I do not love. I do not linger. Why distinguish what I think from what I do, thought Curzon. One day I shall be able to gratify my longing to act in my own times – to perform some specific act of anticipation … to work for the proletariat … But not yet. Not while I am so useless …)

How snug, in the last redoubt, with one's last lake of wine to drink down, to watch the children struggling down from the hot winy slopes with fresh baskets of pleasure. And I'd not care if this were apomorphine or whatever, except that there would be no drug bars as there are no drug stores. The only problem here is that after nine o'clock, the respectable or the careful people come in. 'Let me not be drunk when I leave,' they say. Why choose the horse one is to ride home on when the stables are full? Much wittier to select from two, or three, indeed, and to suggest that one would be different if one could.

(Where am I when I think? thought Curzon, tipping down more wine.)

'People who buy pictures confront the artists with hostility in that they wish to buy his work as cheaply as possible without in fact enquiring how much he has sold. To be just, one should assume full responsibility for less successful artists, paying them all one has for the tiniest sketch. I certainly do not propose to haggle when attracted by a work of art.'

They were sitting by a sacred stream, where scabby goats were playing. Little girls came and offered basil and other branches of herb to make a couch. Curzon was tired of smelling like a stuffed roast chicken: one of the seven kings of Bihar slowly passed by in his yacht. Or perhaps it was not he.

'One talks cheerfully of discontinuities in time and so on, when dealing with political systems and the like – but in real life one does not suddenly slide off the end of a week into next month. Though I suppose when one steps out of the tourist bus into the mosque one steps from capitalism into contemplation – and yet one carries around one's fetishism notwithstanding. "Will they steal my shoes if I leave them outside?" and so on.

'In fact, on the whole I should prefer, when I move from one system to another, change dialectical modes in midstream, step back a few centuries, as the guides say – or take another look at life soon – to see the calendar swiftly change. Far from time and space providing a self-consistent framework which makes the other discontinuities and our own business life easy to reconcile, I find time and space as we seem to have them, ridiculous and dysfunctional.

'If only when we go to the airport and book to Benares, the clerk would say, "Do you wish to go by a measure of sociocultural time or sociocultural space? And will you be changing yourself, or go as you are?'

'These herbs have beetles. They are green-gold and red.'

'In the dark all beetles are black.'

The mounted artillery band went 'Crump, crump, crump' as

the ministers climbed up the stairs. The marble pillars looked like disagreeable corned beef or brawn. One of the delegates felt a tingling in his arm and some elation without motive – and determined that if he was in for a bout of brain haemorrhage or syncope, he would take care to immiserate a lot of people first. At this point of the pyramid, he reflected, the system is translated into quality – into an individual whose only need is to exist. For a moment he thought he was going to tumble down the stairs again, clumsy and stiff as an umbrella. Would the band stop?

He turned to his companion and asked, 'What happens if one of us dies?' and giggled.

No one heard his question. Searching the dying waves with the tuning needle late at night, hearing ten countries extinguishing themselves with national anthems, he searched the faces of the others, already in his imagination set in indifference to his death.

Hop hop through the grass went a fine pair of toads. There was lilac drooping in beard-shapes over a small marble cistern where lute players came in the evenings and sang of their lovers, sweet-sharp as apricots or lynxes. We are not yet attuned to the bicameral system, politely explained the peasants to their ex-colonial masters when these returned as tourists. We don't in any case find it necessary to have politics.

However, the imperial power had not suggested that trade unions were a useful barrier to protect the population from the inertia of its legislature, nor had it provided its imperial peoples with a party system based on class interests as its own were. Consequently, miners were to be seen crawling round the villages with their crushed hindquarters strapped to boards with children's rollerskate wheels at the corners. (No, thought Curzon, this is not yet when I mean – but we are surely coming closer.)

Two cats were rolling in a heap of basil which had been gathered for the seven sleeping silver fish trapped that morning. On the rough surface of the town square a fleet of twenty harvesters was being refuelled from cans before attacking the surrounding cornlands, while loudspeakers played the Great Fugue. A man was painting his house blue. Four youths were watching a foal being sold to a man in black sheepskins and a conical hat of bown fur.

'Don't you find all this exciting?' asked Curzon.

'Not in the same way as you do – a way I find rather frightening. To me these are illustrations of a possible way of life, which I might come to admire and belong to, but which has at the moment only the most superficial significance for me. You, however, see these flashes of existence and relationship as an aspect of life more intense, more valid, and in a sense more intellectually satisfying than any logical relationship, more enlightening than any concept.

'It frightens me that you are at once able to connect, and to romanticise, with such alien and half-understood glimpses of other people's lives, and so deeply – and yet so unable to give a shape and direction to your own life, so reluctant to make contact with those you like and who like you. Perhaps you are right to be afraid that there is something nasty or deficient, just below the surface of your closed little personality.'

No, I know where this ends, thought Curzon, snails who come a short way out of their shells are either set upon by salt, or simply want to move about from one leaf to another. Or is it salt that snails have to fear? Animals with soft skin, a poor turn of speed and a great deal of bony baggage to cart about should stay indoors as much as possible. If only, thought Curzon, I could invent a reality which, in my imagination, I did not dominate ...

The letter – covered with the passing thoughts of a score of censors and policemen, the flute melodies of a couple of postmen – how many Balkan songs rely on the letter for vital communications between lovers! Letters bringing news too of Uncle Branko being hanged on a bridge, and Radoman going as a soldier and blowing himself up on the first day. Letters always falling short of the real desires, or expressing interest where there is none: only later do the letters crystallise relationships which have never existed and could never otherwise exist. On the marble table is a pool of maraschino and one calls for beer to wash the sticky sweet from one's head.

Sometimes in this race across Europe weeks and cities would pass as if they were single frames in an interminable film. Time and place were conflated, cultural history was displaced into Curzon's private perception and memory, so that events like the burning of Tienen, the Turkish occupation, mingle with the beer and the marc and the sitting up in trains at night with roundels of privacy, misty silver dollars of nostalgia and obscure anniversary, roundels of warm breath on train windows.

Much of the time they were drunk, passing from one country to another – or indeed one century to another. Elizabeth denied having travelled in a balloon in her life.

'Isn't it true,' asked Curzon, 'that Lenin said in the Stockholm Co-op when being pressed to buy more clothes, "I'm going to Petrograd to start a revolution, not a gentlemen's outfitters"? And if that is an uninventable truth – then surely you are convinced that we were lucid in the blank patches between countries?'

But they could never find Tienen on the map. 'Proves nothing,' said Curzon. 'The dialectic is a hard bird to pluck, but it struts about all right.'

'Above all,' said Elizabeth,'we should be grateful that the details of our lives have not lingered on to the end. If one believes in any kind of flow of communication, one should surely be able to swan around the civilised and recorded world – avoiding imagined corners for all one's worth – without leaving the library. I put this forward as an explanation in lieu of a hypothesis. It certainly explains that series of Sundays we caught – you remember, we could never shake off a convoy of popes?'

'Five shillings a song,' said the lad with the bagpipe outside their hotel.

'I suppose successive layers of guilt, and idleness, and stubbornness, form a hard case around the original lively transmitter. Instead of outgoing as on wishes, for reasons probably of excessive sensitivity – or the inadequate receptiveness of others – the transmitter takes to sending either short and runic cries for help, or sends out in memory-dots pictures of human beings to people on other planets. This may mean that there's some irritating fault in the receiving equipment, some structural fault in circuit design, or even in electrical conceptualising. Or it may mean only that the operator of the transmitter is unwilling or unable to spend hours finding the correct frequency – or that he finds the other transmitters cluttered with racing results. By the way, how boring that racing should be between like things – or at most between bicycles and runners, dogs and horses: how splendid to have races between the Gay Nineties, Genghiz Khan and primitive accumulation. To see not which one of them wins, but which of us ...'

'Yes, yes – enough of that, surely. But can't you see your not liking me sufficiently reflects just that – an insufficiency, not an inadequacy?'

How odd, thought Curzon, that to be let off an awkward relationship requires an act of niceness which makes the parting possible and yet by that very token unwelcome. Let me sort myself out, thought Curzon:

'Imagine these two, bound by their class, restricted by traditions in which they live uneasily and without conviction, prevented by taste and reason from defending the privileges they despise – and which in any case are slipping away. And yet the choice before them is either to defend the palaces, the aristos in their Bugattis, the tidal filth and ancestral sediment which has fed and nauseated them, or to accept the slow transformation of the past which, after all, has fed them like rich mud, into a thin, eroded painfully cultured soil.

'They have no place with their class, no professional talent forever at the service of the barbaric tides from the steppes: they have grown up sickly with self-doubt, self-disgust, but they cannot enjoy the destruction of their plush nursery toys.

'Their consciousness, and rejection, of their class affiliation inhibits their enjoyment of conjecture – and their search for emancipation. The only possibility is to leave – to jumble the tokens in the game that nanny taught once and for ever: the counters, the symbols of the players, have been lost and replaced with cabuchons and hazel nuts, cartridges and wrist bones. But the game remains – perhaps by sitting in the garden where hoopoes strut about every noon, playing tric-trac, one can change the rules of the game and the stakes.'

But, thought Curzon, I can't do this splendid trick if Elizabeth is here. To accept that accession of personality which loving her involves is to tie me – I must break these filaments or stay rooted to the spot.

'But, my darling,' said Elizabeth, 'if you base your life on rejecting the contacts you need, you want – you're comic, pathetic. What's the use of saying the international proletariat shall be the human race, or whatever, when you're just exchanging one historical necessity – which you see through and have resisted – for another, to which you wish to become subservient, for which you want to die, want to have to die. It's either wrong or comic – because you're ceasing to be a person, you're becoming a slave to someone else's history.'

The eyes painted on the prow of the boat sought out a pale-green mosque in a corner of the lake. A man in the stern managed at last to find Radio Kabul on his transistor, and a song about tulips came and went on the elastic radio miles. Discarded nursery donkeys stood about on the steps.

Lily-roots caught at the keel, and they noticed two little girls rowing a huge lily leaf into the centre of the lake. 'Let's get off here – we can ride back in a De Soto if we're lucky.

Mind the bones. I hope you don't object to the smell of hashish?'

They walked among the tombs where a few old men were smoking delightedly. A man with a silver pheasant in the crook of his arm was lying in wait for yellow grasshoppers.

'While I was young,' said Curzon, 'I thought all I had to do to make people malleable was to emerge from my ennui periodically and chat to them. I would say that, determinist though I was, by providing them with a brief social confrontation, I would ensure a complete correspondence between them and me. I assumed for years that everyone was like everyone else, face to face, and if anyone maintained anything else, they must for obscure reasons be lying.

'Later, when I realised that this was absurd and that no one was talking to me, I concluded that I was so wild and exotic (like everyone else), that one encountered other people flashing past at just below the speed of light. One was just able to raise a hand – perhaps to gesticulate, blow a kiss, or deliver a quick curse – but one's social speed was so enormous that one never realised what effect, if any, one's flagging and signalling had on other people.

'One was always at the crossroads, there were always an infinite number of old men and Oedipuses grinding out their last cigarettes as one toiled up the hill in the hot sun preparing some myth for the asking. This meant that one was always face to face with one's own, or someone else's destiny; always answering some damned riddle or other – never finishing with curing the plague of this good lady, or handing out fully-researched material on blight for the people in the corner house. And this grew tedious.

'And so I turned to politics. This desperate wish to slow down the rush of conjecture to suit my own more modest pace by finding a firm theoretical basis against which to meet my inevitable martyrdom ...'

Elizabeth dropped some frangipani on a lizard. 'Since you are clearly infatuated with yourself – or at best a social cripple among social cripples,' she said, 'I suppose I must not split myself with laughing at the incongruity of my chase after you to the far side of the dialectic. You manage to make the rest of us limp like you – and then you straighten up, and say "End of joke", and you're off to the wings for a quick giggle with the chorus. And the rest of us are left with the malady you perceived in us – or passed on to us, for all I know. And even that would be all right, if you cared a little: but all you want is to swan around. Do you remember telling us your ambition? "To get drunk in a public house in London before ten in the morning, legally?"'

'You're so right, Elizabeth dear. Up to a point, and with a thousand reservations.'

Across the road in the Fascist Local, a man was lying on the dirtiest bed in the world drinking the tenth beer of the morning. In 'Man's Hope', the bar next door, the clerks from the conveyancing office were playing tric-trac. Last month's olive oil groped up the wall of the hotel like a stain. In the yard below Curzon's window a nest of unusable tomatoes looked like the spawn of red frogs. A smell of stale goulash, thin old dogs and body makeup of the 1890s hung just outside the balcony like a curtain.

In this inert little community, only one man was working –

beating ploughshares into ploughshares.

'What a foul little town this is,' said Elizabeth.

'Positively our last appearance. We survivors from Teinen must, however, be careful about the judgement we pass. I believe there's an interesting Manichean cathedral here: there are enough Armenians left here for some interesting chitter-chat. It's the malaria that makes everyone seem a bit *distrait*. Tomorrow we'll go up to the hills. Sandy goat pastures: last judgments by a variety of crude hands in pine churches. Dead horses in the riverbeds unfurling like dismasted brown and white umbellas.'

'Pig.'

A transcontinental truck from Bulgaria pulled slowly up the main street, but did not stop: Curzon and Elizabeth wished that it would. A policeman came out of Man's Hope and fell two or three times on the pavement outside.

'Unravelled,' he shouted up to them. 'You may think you're free of my malice up there. But as God made the planets, I'll drink you down like the wine of remembrance. My little kittens.' He sat enjoying the sticky yellow bubble he had bought for his interior, and which was now fitted like a second and more efficient ribcage, stopping the heart and stomach rubbing together.

'I feel like some of that myself,' said Curzon. 'It seems like the right stuff.'

This is the ultimate in boredom and melancholia, and it's mine, all mine, he thought. So, my life has become a destiny – everything I think, is. So there's no hope but the Man's Hope. Down where the caperings of tired barmen are pressing out the last lucent berries for the last lucent customers. Summoning up the last of my zest for life, I'll bellow "Join me in a large one." What a monstrous appetite for new social experience. I'll put all the unanswered questions to sleep in my sunny swash of one two three bottles. Nice to know that Elizabeth can't follow me down this rat's hole.

'I wish I could lick this paranoia,' said Curzon, after a bottle or two in Man's Hope.

'No, you're correct,' said Elizabeth, 'they are watching us.'

'Can it be they've never seen two faded old drunks before? I'd have thought tourists here left looking like shreds of wallpaper.' Curzon hummed a few partisan songs, which he had always heard unlocked deep private cellars, full of remorse-free wine.

'What will become of us?' wondered Curzon hopefully. 'Perhaps we'll burst into disalienation at the point of a bayonet.'

A dark red cat smelling of thyme lay down on their table.

Eventually, one of the clerks came over. 'You are a socialist?' he asked Curzon.

'Of a kind – but of that kind, yes, thoroughly and consciously a socialist.'

'Tell us about your socialism: we have never met a foreign socialist scholar before, and we should like to hear all you can tell us of your beliefs and the points at which they may help us.

'I am Sadik. My parents send me abroad to university, and when I returned I could not be employed because my opinions were not amenable to security – they would not take me into the army without a security check, they would not even check me, and if I did not go into the army, I would be arrested as a deserter. So I had to go to the country – as a letter-writer in the provinces. When I came back from France, I was a student, but they have made me a communist, and I am grateful.

'In the provinces I used to live on the melon which had not been pared away from the skin – there were scores of us scavengers, with a more or less respectable legal existence as tutors, writers, letter-writers, artists and so forth. But I was the only man who tried to organise the other scavengers, the unemployed, the crippled workers. The men from the mines used dynamite when they lost their jobs – and they were the first to train me. I spent a year living under the stage in a little theatre in the park, and a year living in an attic in the roof of a railway station. After this, I was too ill to go into the army – so I was never tried as a deserter, I was never cleared by security, and I could never get a job. Here in the port, I work in the restaurant for my food.'

He seemed a delicate, a diffident man, one of the thousands of workers whose tuberculosis muted the dockside activity, gave the drinkers an air of convalescence, and encouraged a kind of weary preciseness in everything they said. But his hands were grained with black powder, and as he smiled and talked about the last emir, and the evolution of dance forms, he kept saying 'and when we are in the mountains', 'when we develop our organisation in the interior', 'when the coercive structure of the cities has been sapped ...'

Osman had come to the port as a child, spending all his life as a labourer on the work of building the wooden towers surrounding the docks – once water towers, but now used for storing sunflower seeds, feathers, amber. He had a wide local reputation for composing ghazals – but his union had sent him abroad, rather as Belgian, Spanish, Italian unions had sometimes helped artists sixty years before, and he had lived for some months in Cuba.

Osman and Sadik were the nucleus of the political committee.

'Then of course in the mountains there are the tribes.' The young man called them 'les tribus' which seemed somehow to make them more homogenous and certainly more impenetrable. 'But now,' he continued, 'let me show you the exercise called "Let us close the gaps." Formerly, there used to be a dance in which five soloists would run through a rather elliptical series of dance ideas: then they would work out a way to combine the various figures – bird tree, Austrian March and Mehter, little lily and so on – into one. That man over there – he escaped from Distomon, in Greece, where the Germans killed hundreds of villagers.'

Elizabeth and Curzon walked around the dancers: 'Now, we try to give the dance some political significance. We all feel rather in a backwater here – this town is so provincial. Some of us are communists, some syndicalists: we have some Bakuninists – even one or two "friends of Otto Bauer". We hope that you can drag us up to date, without doing too much of a violence to our objectives.'

'What are these objectives then?'

'That you must see for yourself, when we go to the mountains. The trade unions down here on the coast are no good: the pressures are just too great. But in the mountains there are mining camps, small industrial towns, peasant communes – the lot poised like golden snow, waiting for the right theory, the right movement, the right conjuncture of crises – you must tell us which ...'

Pehraps, after all, this is the place, and the situation, thought Curzon, remembering, however ...

Two Albanians ahead of them down the road were arguing over whose turn it was to sing the next song. On the mountain plateau of Montenegro men were still swapping horses and galloping towards the sun, arms flung wide, hoing to the horse as if to urge it over a prison wall – and yet in pleasure, for they felt free. A man in prison on the coast, who was allowed one of the warder's dogs in his cell to keep him company, rested his chin beside the animal's on the window ledge.

Together they warched tourists walking round the city walls – the roof tiles like toast in the five o'clock sun – saw a Turk fastening a small offering, an empty cigarette packet, to the ground floor bars, in case any friends should pass by.

'Only another month, and it's back to the extended family, and nothing but goats and rent to talk about. What will we do without each other, Milo?' The dog thought no coherent or communicable thoughts.

And for the last time Curzon retreated into his own head ...

On the roof of the station stood four flame-coloured birds; disdainful and goitrous they seemed forever excluded from the merry musical culture of the monkeys, who thought for hours what amusing things they could do with the butts of their bananas. The monkeys had taken to pillaging the temples on whose floors they had been born and bred, and would walk around monklike with feet and fingers of statues – torn off the old ones, or made by themselves in crude imitation.

The gods seemed to have expanded as their temples fell

down: they were now looming above the ruins, like old men in the bath. Some were hugely disfigured with lichens and fungus, vivid green scars eaten into the baked clay-coloured flesh. But they were so massive, and supplied with enough arms and legs to last several lifetimes, that as fast as a monkey would wrench off a limb, a vigorous fungus would grow on the stump. Some statues had been virtually reconstructed of vegetables, all parasitic on each other. In the airfield on the other side of a symmetrical mountain crested with a wattle of pink trees, American airmen were painting flowers on the bombs they were to use the next day. And the birds stood on the roof of the station and thought about nothing.

In the distance the floating capital was being towed out to sea, apparently as if never to come back. Far out at sea, the inshore marine life, which followed the houseboats, the floating town halls, pubs, fire stations, taxi-dance halls, and lived in the scum on their keels, was peeled off by big fish.

'How can we stop you little yellow gets going commie,' mused the American colonel as he watched some villagers preparing to cut up a marrow four yards long.

'Stop that, you goddam monkeys,' he shouted, as they pelted him with fruit and, perhaps, the eggs of the birds on the roof. The largest marrow for thirty miles was much more interesting to the villagers than the monkeys: today, Tuesday, was for general rural pursuits, monkey-training was for Mondays.

*

Curzon asked, 'How can I help this sea of people find a collective personality when I've no particular identity myself? Who am I to say "Bauer did this" or "Trade unions can do that"? Who am I to get these things moving? Who am I?'

'What in fact would Bauer have said?' Elizabeth asked.

'Assuming I've not just invented Bauer, he would say: "To help those who are not socialists re-integrate their social and political lives in the new system which we call socialist is the only free and positive work that a man can do. This solves all the intellectuals' problems of what the intellect can do in society, and all the workers' problems as to the meaning and purpose of their political work.'

'That sounds all right.'

'Of course it does – it's tautologous through and through, and begs any possible question. It is just another of Bauer's jokes. He meant get on and work for something you believe in intellectually and see how it comes out – and conversely think about something you wish to do, and see how much comes. This in fact is what he meant by re-integration.'

And to himself Curzon thought, poor tedious Elizabeth. Never a joke: the sacred monkeys gibbering away like fun, and never a smile from her. Here we all are, making mazes for her, inlaying the family kemanche with a wordplay to enliven the longer passages of strumming – but there's not a smile.

How can she live with a once-for-all ration of such pure tedium? Even drinking bores her – there's nothing new for her in every bottle. 'What's that – a picture?' she asks of a picture. 'Why is that man wearing a hat and carrying one?' – all the detail which in a mass freshens up the to-and-fro of nothing in particular she describes and isolates, so that one realises that whatever unlikely things people are doing around the place, the enormous majority are scraping along in the usual way, without two thoughts among the dozen of them.

'Who are the main enemies, then?' asked Curzon.

'The CCB: we call them "The Criminal Conspiracy of the Bourgeoisie". They call themselves "Class Collaborationists against Barbarism". It's very Chestertonian – but in fact from the legions of thugs to the chiefs of the corporations who fix the price lists for "doing people over", costing social reforms to see if they would affect the infrastructure, the front runs through all classes and is at once composed of the most dynamic leaders of corporations and the most brutalised of the petty criminals. It's a sort of paradigm of society – weighted and made respectable by all those with their heads in the clouds and their feet in the status quo. We find them so strong that, despairing of cracking their defences, we propose leaving the town and devising a strategy up there. This may be a foolish thing – but we cannot bear to see the dockers fight for an increase, win when exhausted, and go cheerfully back to loading war materials which will be used against out comrades elsewhere.'

'But why ask a man like me, from a country where I have known only betrayal, to be your Lenin? Or whatever?'

'We would rather not have a Lenin, please. We have not thought out and fully agreed what are the alternatives. We really want your analysis: if it seems good, and if your premise is that you must be our Lenin, we'll think again.'

Curzon and Elizabeth were left alone. 'You must go,' said Elizabeth. 'All this slipping from country to country and century to century has now stopped: it's the divide between the pretence of searching and the pretence of escaping. But what would Bauer have said?'

'Bauer said, "If I believe what I write, I must come when those for whom I write call me. Why do they never call me? Because they have never heard of me? Why then do I not go where they can know what I am saying? Is it because I do not want to have anyone appeal to me? Do I just wish to be correct and avoid the commitment which might both validate my hypothesis and destroy me? The fact remains that if I am not appealed to, then my writing has failed, and that if my writing succeeds then I will be summoned, and I must go."'

'And did they call?'

'You know very well – he was killed for a cause he detested, led by men he despised and fired on by his friends. He saw this as a punishment for going to an unjust war – but that did no one much good. Categorically ... Yes, I suppose I have no choice. If I'm not strong enough to stand by my beliefs alone, perhaps I'll get on better with this lot.'

A man with a kemanche was singing:

'The thousand jigsaws of the mind
Indented like maps
(This drink is killing me)
Let's fit the countries together!
(But gives a roundness to the maps.)'

'And I can't even speak the language,' grumbled Curzon.

Marvellous! he thought. Another bit of life scraped through – and I've escaped that long stretch of boredom. Free and nothing – gorgeous. Back to the life of afternoon news-theatres, drinking pints of jogurt to live to be two hundred, drinking the green wine in the bars by the opera. Going for the last act – lying like a purring bee in the rope cradles over the stage, and having chirrups and heroic snatches of Janáček swimming up round me. A life in a society where one has a universal laissez-passer – hold the two halves together and you can go anywhere – separate them, and one half lets you experience the passage of time without the friction and attrition this normally involves, the other lets you lie around like a rock pool – a container for other people's busy life.'

And then he remembered that his lassitude was now impermissible.

He watched the fishermen calling 'Vassili, Vassili' to the dolphins. A rusty ship called *The Daughter of Byzance* was wallowing in the middle of the straits. The pilot and the captain were arguing: Curzon could see their arms waving. He asked the waiter, 'Do you have Krk?' The waiter was away for a long time and said he had none, but in such a way as to leave doubt as to whether he knew what Krk was.

A party of burghers and their wives stopped some dock labourers dancing in the garden of the restaurant. 'Go home to your wives, you pigs,' said one of the wives, for all wives. The musicians ironically doffed their tall white conical hats, riding off on donkeys.

TWO

AND SO Curzon left, alone, for 'les tribus'. In the afternoon, the proletarian nation followed – flowers behind the horses' ears, flowers in the spokes of the gun-carriage wheels, flowers in the shotguns carried by the contingent of railwaymen. A band in felt boots shuffled along with gongs and double-trumpets. A policeman threw down his gunbelt and joined the procession.

'We should like to join you,' shouted a group of young paratroopers. Some dockers stopped work to give the popular front salute. The great banners lurched upwards through the orange groves: twenty or thirty railway workers, still covered in flowers, still wearing little wreaths of basil, sheepishly came back to town just after dark. The police questioned some of them, but only a few were beaten.

In a day and a half of clambering over the rocks above the town, all but forty had given up. Those who returned to the town spoke of the need for a correct theory before setting out again, and often wished the survivors of the first day's procession well – but they never overcame their antipathy towards Curzon. The townsmen could see for weeks the crimson wings of the banners abandoned among the magnolias on the lower slopes.

Figments, like lizards, ran to be chopped in the road by the camions of the gendarmes.

'And so,' thought Curzon, 'we're out of the country of the people with no memories. Class and caste are nicely conflated here. There's no problem of some wealthy and liberal government having to justify itself before its citizens as it frizzles me up at the head of my band of peasants – at the cost of great expense and suffering to itself, of course. There's no point in political scientists developing a counter-ideology to my own, categorising my movement into the ephemeral or unfree – with what precision, what lingering late over the brandy and the card-index. The only subjective element in the present struggle can be fear.'

'To go back after twenty years,' he said, 'and discover exactly where one got the image of red and blue brick walls, the lane down which, notionally, one had to make a life's journey before going to sleep each night – this shows one at the fork of an evolving tree. Like a lemur, one inches back down the branch to the starting point, And always a girl in blue – of the age I was when I left, always a girl in blue to whom I feel drawn, always, though, a girl who has no memory of me or of my desire—'

'Is she veiled, this girl?'

'Of course not.'

'Is she a communist?'

'I very much doubt it.'

'Is she of the bourgeoisie?'

'I imagine so.'

'How good to know our fortunes are in the hands of a fantasist …'

But Curzon's fantasies were behind him, where the others had theirs to come. And that evening Curzon outlined the dimensions of their commissary for the first three months.

The walks of the city were made of mud, with a facing of glazed clay bricks, turquoise, blue – in stiff patterns struggling to become words, 'As is', 'if is' and their mirror versions. Inside the walls, desert. Then stockades where the peasants left their donkeys. Then an outer ring of tea houses, where men in caftans ate melon while their wives stood about inside in the sun – silver, purple, green, and gold painted on the silk like bands of feathers. Men in felt boots walked through the market to play billiards in a converted mosque: many held wooden eggs with leather strings fastened to one end. All day a hot, gritty wind blew in from the deserts which surrounded the city. In the square, a black dog, split open by a truck, snarled at his own tripes.

There was little to sell but melons and sunflower seeds. A Turkoman was singing a song to the dutar about a cockerel he had been accused of stealing. Some men from les tribus pooled their money to buy one of their number some tea and grapes. The other peasants stared at him with enough intensity to make him feel awkward, but not enough to convey hostility.

Sadik tried to explain and describe what Curzon could see and hear.

'Those were men from out of town. The word you didn't understand is a corrupt Persian word for landlord. They don't really understand what or who they pay rent to – whether it's the government, a bailiff, the landlord himself – or whether 'landlord' itself is just another name for history, or fate, or bad luck or whatever. They asked if we'd come like the Russians to tell them to refuse their rent.'

'But there can have been no Russians here for years. They'd have been spotted.'

'In 1907 some of the Russian railway workers came this way – they'd been working on the line to Kazan. The people round about have never forgotten. They think you are a Russian.'

'What did you tell them?'

'I told them yes – you have come to tell them not to pay rent, and to tell them you wish them also to chase the landlords from the town where they live.'

'But I'm not sure about the peasants yet. And anyway, even if we intended a premature rising, this is ridiculous. I'm supposed to be the theoretician.'

'You obviously don't understand how an idea like the one I've given them works. For two generations – more – they've known exactly what a revolution should mean to them. They have had sixty years of discussion and education. They only want some kind of trigger, some kind of purpose.'

'Is this what you meant when you said in building up the urban cadres we are not producing leaders and philosophers, but re-educating clerks to be our clerks?'

'The townsmen here need all the classes you can give them in theory, loyalty, memory work. Most of their life has been an attempt to escape from politics and economics, to rise through the police or the civil service by the strength of their ambition.

You've to deflect them from the course of a lifetime – their desire to stay alive, to dominate, not to die of tuberculosis, not to annoy their employers. For the peasants, there's no escape: even the prosperous peasants are dangled on the end of their prosperity by the landlord, like a mouse being held over a cliff by its tail. You won the peasants when you arrived.

'What will happen in the next months is that they will drift away, in disillusion, or because their rivalry comes to seem more immediately important than their shared exploitation – or again because you are unsuccessful or because someone gets at them. But by morning, you will have a notional army of several hundreds in the mountains, who will have been waiting for you for a hundred years. The only difference is that now the old social structures of les tribus have been undermined and eaten through by the landlords. The peasants have a motive now for coming into the towns. And they've no crops that the women can't cope with – their families now have not enough land for everyone to have work on it, and the police turn them away from the towns.'

'Why do you believe you belong here?'

'I would not make a profession like that. I belong because I have to take the consequences of being about the place. I have no privilege, I am totally involved, wholly responsible, and completely defenceless.'

They slipped propaganda in melon skins and sold them by the thousand as charms. Fig merchants wrapped their sticky sweets in pamphlets and Tajiks sucked them all the way to their farms. By ingestion, by osmosis, by illiterates scraping the revolutionary glyphs on walls, by schemes of land reform given away as paper fans and issued as bus tickets – the cities of the interior buzzed with politics and rising consciousness, like pots of golden bees.

The rivers were green with frogs that spring, and the straw gods which had guarded the wine jars throughout the winter were carried down to the water's edge to frighten off the lynxes. Generals from the capital came to gallop through the suburbs, crammed into corsets and cuirasses, or were driven down the main street, crying 'Faster, faster,' to the chauffeurs.

'We must consolidate all this,' said Curzon. 'All this must be organised, and we must get the gods burned.'

'Nonsense – later, perhaps, if it is necessary. We can hide arms in the mosques and propaganda in the gods. We need all the cover we can find,' said the political committee.

'But I've done nothing – no analysis, no theory, no leadership.'

'None was necessary. You were the detonator. You gave us the confidence we needed to leave the port, to seek the interior – we didn't need to import you: you belonged to the port, and now you have become a memento. We are with the strength of the movement – with the cities of the interior, with the farmers, and with les tribus. This is our basis. When we win, you will be essential. Now you can help only to keep us close to the movement – the movement itself, though, is in existence, and you can't change it, damage it, improve it, at this stage. Every tea-house of the city, every peasant on his donkey, is wholly taken up with new ideas, blowing in under the eyelids and fingernails like dust from the walls and the desert.'

'But our revolution must not turn sour: we must never find ourselves in a position of hostility to our rank and file.'

'We try and we hope: but at the moment we and the movement are one.'

Already men were painting murals by night of 'The dialectic entering the capital on the back of a lynx', covering them up with plaster to be stripped off when the day at last arrived.

From the air they could see, in the tan desert, roads which stopped in curious farmyards without soil or animals, networks of waterless trenches and nicely squared plots of gravel. Sometimes there were animal tracks limping off into the sand, and they could even see the heaps of brocade and silk where groups of expropriated peasants had wandered off along the desert roads in the hope of a lift to the towns, and died in the first few hours of their short cuts.

Sadik proposed that all their organisations should have shadow forms – as it were, a secret drawer in every committee, a false bottom in every cadre. For a time they used a circus as a front, trying to keep people away by advertising the tameness of their lions, the smallness of their giants, the safety and stiffness of their acrobats – but everyone rushed to enjoy these marvels, and few were disappointed. The cities of the interior had hard circles of refugees in the fields outside the walls, like growth rings on a tree these encampments marked bad harvests and floods, and expropriation. These former peasants were not allowed into the town, and held miserable markets under the walls where they sold the refuse of the citizens

In the mornings, when the more prosperous peasants were allowed into the town market, the dispossessed gathered round, trying to sell portable ovens made of pressed tin cans, melon seeds, patched wine jars, used exercise books, corks, bandages and charms. They were too wretched to interest themselves in politics, too tired to trouble the police. But the government was convinced that they were revolutionaries, and sent troops to garrison the towns. As the price of food in the towns rose, the recruits found they had less to eat, and went off to friends and relations among the surrounding peasants, who taught them insurrectionary songs and insults, and gave them sunflower seeds and a little maize.

The townspeople hated the soldiers, and urged them to leave, preferably after killing the refugees. The officers boasted that they would shortly march against les tribus, but les tribus had informers in the town and their reports led the tribesmen to move down the mountains into the lemon groves, which they then fortified.

Sadik and Curzon spent most of their time in the underground section of a medieval observatory – perched on a marble and obsidian sextant. Lizards came in there for a rest, and on the walls were sequences from 'the dreams of Uluk', 'Woodrow Wilson as a winged victory' and 'how the tiger helps the sun rise'. It was a good place to discuss the dialectic, and they found the girls from les tribus who worked as couriers quick at differentiating between dialectical modes – and scented with mace and apples.

Sadik described the festivals of les tribus – festivals of the lynx, and the more self-indulgent ones of frogs and melons – festivals used more to repel the inquisitive than to initiate the young. At night, Curzon could hear soft laughter as men raced their lynxes and flew their flaming kites by the hundred over the desert. The girls would stay sometimes to sing in the observatory – sweetly taunting Sadik and Curzon for sitting about all day in a cave full (or so they speculated) of dynamite and sovereigns. The girls were sharp as quinces – sometimes they danced a shuffling desert dance, panting languidly in evocation of their native altitude, moving like living silk poured out, at once too amazed and too wise to bother with gravity.

Soon Sadik was as alarmed as Curzon that the girls might be caught. The girls themselves expected this: perhaps to them the observatory, with its smell of gun-oil, the two men arguing and slicing melons, the furtive dances and the whispered ghazals and chirrups of song, was already in part a prison.

'Why are you called les tribus?' asked Curzon.

'It's a name. Some peasants who leave their land go to the towns, or live outside them, others go to the mountains, the desert, the steppe – like us. We wouldn't pay taxes, so we race lynxes.'

'And fly burning kites. And starve to death.'

'And, Curzon, have for generations known about the things you want to tell us – long before the men came from Kazan. Our culture lies in the desert – pink and blue mosques, libraries – it's all a few feet under the sand. We collect the clean pieces, we learn the most pleasant epics – but we don't grovel down into the mountains of dead bones, we don't excavate and restore. We just lift off what is movable. We have no feelings for dead people – but we're rightly suspicious of dead things, that is, we can't carry much with us. We have to be refined – there's so much of other people's history underfoot we have to take great care to pick up only what is portable.'

Occasionally, Sadik would go into the city, telling monstrous lies about the movement's strength and weakness, and the location of its strong points. The nervousness which imminent guerrilla attack brought on affected the scavengers and the artists most acutely. The streets soon piled high with refuse, and the refugees lived so well that they began to raise themselves to a full awareness of their misery – for the street cleaners were on strike against the danger from attacks yet to be launched. The rubbish saturated and undermined the clay houses, and the whole city began to tilt and sag. The river looked oily and the donkeys would not drink from it. A boat festival could not be held because the performers complained that their oars could not be forced into the viscous water, and that the stench of the river made them feel ill when they were wearing their carnival heads.

A similar collapse affected the writers: they used words of English, Old Persian canting slang, mysterious abbreviations, and blundered glottal versions of an archaic demotic. The artists painted away like so many golems – bridal fantasies, the end of planets, Woodrow Wilson entering heaven on a tiger – a mass of local nonsense, misunderstood metropolitan symbology and so forth. It was as if a great rich tide of sewage had come bubbling up from the central fountain in the imperial baths. Only the girls from les tribus watched the dissolution of the body politic into a broth of warm brawn with detachment and sympathy.

And yet, as Sadik pointed out, all they had done so far was to organise the more sophisticated, call on the ancestral memories of les tribus and the peasants, and let it be known, more or less by spontaneous rumour, that this time the insurrection would be planned and well-armed. So far men had not assumed from this that if the revolution succeeded on such a basis it would of necessity run the risk of being more coercive than other previous populist risings. And yet at the first touch, the city gave off a splendid puff of decadence, like a dying toadstool giving off spores, collapsing in a babel of little magazines and provincial argots. Phenomenology boomed. Ice cream 'insurrection' was enthusiastically sold: in the 'park without flowers' smoke from the charcoal grills whipped into the eyes and mouths of painted cosmopolitan lieutenants. The domestic electricity supply failed, and men sat on their doorsteps or gossiped under the street lights with an unusual persistence and seriousness. Those who had no electricity brought naphtha lamps and paraffin flares into the street junctions and laughed and danced into the night.

'The hardest thing, it seems to me, is to go in search of the key to one's past, the figure in the nursery carpet and so forth – exhume the teddy bears, rebuild the battle kit of the soldiers – without letting this search dominate one's perceptions of broader historical forces. And, indeed without letting these forces interrupt the seeking for the inner rationality, the visceral cause and effect, those factory processes of the metabolism which distil now a sip of acid, now a long draught of some herbal nonsense. I think we're looking for an unanswerable indictment, rather than a case to answer.'

'Surely this is nonsense,' said Sadik. 'Nice nonsense. It's too late to unravel your past from your memories, and to sort out the future you want from the past you fear. None of this matters now, because you're with les tribus, you depend on me, my loyalty, the judgement, the humour, the integrity, of the political committee – just as we all depend on you. This is the intersection of all our past lives – and the only concern is that you should at this moment be trustworthy, sober and confident. Your lost time is of no interest even to yourself – at best it accounts for deficiencies in your activity at present, and we will help you to overcome these. You are as deeply committed now to us – and we to you – as you were to yourself. In your better moods, you realise this makes you stronger, just as it balances your life over a more perilous crevasse.'

*

The period of legality – spent in the underground observatory, or on the fringe of the desert – seemed to Curzon to last for years. The exotic and symbolic surroundings and activities, the learning of Persian terms for cotton-spinning processes, the teasing by the girls from les tribus – all this was exhausting and bewildering. The intensity of the excitement was increased by the confluence of festivals in the city. The railwaymen prepared to celebrate 'the visitors from Kazan' and enclosed the locomotives in an armour of scarlet wood.

In a tent, fifty people were watching an American film. The gunfire from the screen answered the volleys from the troops at practice. Kerosene flares lit the skullcaps of the townsmen and the apricot, lilac and flamingo headcloths of les tribus, as they turned gravely from good to evil and back in the images on the tent wall. Distorted and elongated by the breezes and wrinkles in the canvas screen, the gunmen aspired to three dimensions. The subtitles followed every twig of the plot, and at times of excitement the whole screen was full of comment, explanation and translation in arabic script – the action sometimes even frozen to enable the audience to read the commentary in full. Overhead a fruit tree was dropping husks, and occasionally a small green monkey would scamper over the tent gathering the fruit. The film with its concordance moved stiffly, the action protracted and turned into concepts, the to-and-fro of life proceeding without comment and often at an absurd speed.

'These scrolls are more interesting for their use of time than the portrayal of people,' a man from les tribus said. 'How long would it take for us – as we are, not in a scroll – to achieve justice? See how quickly these men with guns can resolve disputes …'

There was a murmur of impatience, agreement and uncertainty. Another man said, 'You don't kill the landlord, because he is depth and extent as well as time and character.'

'But the landlord is not immortal – and we of les tribus have no landlord: it is good to be outside the limits of the landlord, but life is even harder. Who could we kill to be free?'

'We have the buried cities, the lynx-races and the flaming kites. To come down to fight in the cities would only mean the townsmen would turn against us.'

'But we know what the peasants and the townsmen have forgotten, or have no time to consider. Our women are free: we have a knowledge of our history which includes the peasant and the townsman – we know more than they.'

'Good, then, let it remain like that. Why help the townsmen to change their masters when this means we shall undergo the mastery of the townsmen?'

'Because the days of les tribus are over: no one will help us to stay guardians of buried libraries, strips of reclaimed desert. We can either take drastic action to shape our future – or see our culture eroded …'

Fifty metres away a spent bullet rapped a bell, and in surprise the monkey lost its hold. The men of les tribus turned back to 'the scrolls'.

Among the reeds water buffaloes poked their heads above the water as if reluctant not to drown. 'That dog is beginning to rot,' said a girl from les tribus, indicating a warm black corpse by the entrance to the observatory. Some men had stacked themselves with drugs for the afternoon, and came leaping, flying, around the swamp on the shoulders of living towers – careful that as they tumbled back into the mud they should not hurt themselves more than was necessary. Sadik and Curzon themselves idly drew up schemes of local government, slipped pamphlets under the skins of melons, and played the pebble game with the couriers from les tribus.

The few trees by the stone-lined reservoirs dropped their leaves – silver, copper-alloy, scarlet – into the green water. Like silver and scarlet leaves the fish – sacred because no one could eat them – sipped at the refuse. As on every hot autumn afternoon, impromptu choirs, ensembles of dutars and doiras, wove their way through undemanding dialogue. Trains of donkeys carrying opium to the American bases limped through the hot sand. Curzon remembered a film he had seen of

Chinese communists being shot one by one by gangs with rifles: for a moment his body winced squeamishly with the imagined convulsions of the dead dog.

How pleasant, after all, to live on as a shy, penniless old man, on a peach a day, a quick chirrup to the sun each morning – a little bread, a lot of melon, surely that would be better than destruction in the prison yard? But this would mean a life of silence, waiting for the onset of uselessness, hearing one's cracked voice bringing out the recurring and forever vital and one-dimensional demands – melon, lynx-racing, apricots, some sour wine. In that silence only that absurdly childish whimper, requesting its food, a joke every now and then, to be allowed to hold the cat – was this really a human destiny, one which could be chosen eagerly?

'I'm sorry,' said Curzon, 'I know all my heresies. It gets tedious sitting here all day, cut off from les tribus and the town.'

'You're in the town,' said Sadik. 'We have six regular couriers from les tribus who will almost certainly be caught before us – and, if you need comfort, if they're caught it will be our fault for being so incautious.'

After this Curzon took a still greater interest in the girls since his fate had been identified with theirs.

'Why should they send us away?' asked Shala. 'If you are not afraid, and we are not – why make an elaborate system of passing messages which involves men from the town?'

'Because the messages go to the town, and come back here, in a straight line. Because the money and arms are hidden around about here. And because foolish mistakes make success less likely.'

But Shala smiled as if success was the least of her problems. Usually she and the other girls asked questions of the order of 'What useless things are you doing today, all day as usual?' and indeed, Sadik and Curzon used only to produce almost illiterate pamphlets on a machine they could not work, to quarrel, and to strip automatic weapons they dared not test, in the hope of discovering if all the parts had been supplied.

But for once Shala said, 'You are not so absorbed and so serious as Sadik. I think you expect us to fail, in one way or another. But we are not creatures of your imagination. We have an interest in ourselves, in our own safety, as deep as yours.'

'Yes, Shala, I know.'

And for once – perhaps because he had been doubting it – he was sharply aware of the responsibility he carried, seeming to cancel out his own dependence and self-doubt. Perhaps, he thought, as the prisoner being put into the cell is freed of his handcuffs. But in fact that custom was not observed locally.

Although they spent several hours each day trying to sort out the shifting relationship between the nucleus of the organised movement, its shadow forms, its fronts, accommodation addresses, lies, breeding and subdividing legal personalities, they were forced to rely on a framework of those who had left the coast and come with them to the interior. These men were as conspicuous in their own way as were the couriers from les tribus. Curzon imagined Shala moving like tracer through the city – and sometimes it seemed that she was instead only a beetle crawling intently through the dust, scarlet wingcases attracting every wheel, every foot.

Please, thought Curzon, let me not overvalue the role of les tribus for the revolution, or for me. Our task must be to develop an armed force, close to the urban unions, fighting, if only incidentally, the battle of the peasants in the battle for the towns. Les tribus is an incidental problem. And for myself, there can be no present with a girl from les tribus.

'Unless les tribus are more in control of us, and more structurally vital, than we believe,' said Sadik. 'Neither Shala nor les tribus will act peripherally just because their activity in your scheme is peripheral. Shala does not act as a courier irrespective of what she sees to be the interest of les tribus – nor independently of her interest in you.'

'But,' said Curzon, 'here's this splendid girl – wild honey, apricots, taming the lynxes—'

'Stop it. Every word you say diminishes her. Of course there is a tide of cross reference, of repeated actions, words, symbols – but all this is of no importance compared with the question of what you are to do in the next few weeks. If Shala is caught, what matters is how much contact with her you can have – not how little. Just as what matters is how much help we can give les tribus – not how small a role they play in our theory. Workers of the world, you know, *proletarii vsyekh stran* – not interconnect mentally but actually rub shoulders. It's easy enough to lose your freedom in the worker's cause, one way or another: you believe the intensity of Shala's life is dangerous, perhaps fatal. She thinks it deeply rewarding – as I do, and as you do for yourself, for your own life. It is, I think, not moral that you deny Shala the fulfilment of a few weeks when you yourself desire this, for however short a time.'

'Yes. I am only slowly realising how much effort commitment to disalienation takes. To accept the possibility of arrest and death is much easier than to take the offer – the necessity – of creative life.'

A small crowd of drunks was feebly trying to overturn some cars. Youths ran and jumped along the roofs of parked cars.

'Lovely!' said a policeman, drawing his baton.

'New life ...' screamed a man, hurling a bottle into the air. Someone sat on a low wall holding his head as blood and arak bubbled from his mouth. Broken glass gleamed up to the circling hawks like rats' eyes. A policeman explained to Osman: 'Casual violence discredits and cheapens revolt – it attracts street rodents. You see that little boy? – I got in two good blows to the shoulder – smashed a collarbone, I reckon. Yes, of course we'd rather not hit people – but you'll admit it's more fun to go for a drunk than some lad with a gun or an injunction.'

Curzon said, 'In England the modes of our bourgeoisie are fairly pacific. I find it odd that people should be prepared to club and be clubbed for the sake of the last half-smile in a bottle of arak.'

'That shows at least how incorruptible you are,' said Osman. Osman operated like a main hinge between the centre in the observatory and the militants in the house of trades in the city. He was easily the most creative of them all – concerned to discover new media of exchange and to materialise relationships at no point susceptible to money. It was becoming clear, in fact, that so far only Osman's programme for the party, his instructions on ‘comradely discipline and comradely cooperation’, and some short poems purporting to be projected back from a time some years ahead, had any claim to be remembered and accounted successful. Sadik’s work of organisation had been intended to run over the city like muscle – but in fact, it was ramshackle. The grand design was fingered out in the streets and markets by the couriers – enjoying their freedom from the desert, from their families, they lived out, figured out in their own elegant and elliptical gestures, a penetrating and inconclusive arithmetic. It was for this reason that Shala’s suggestion that Curzon should go to the protection of les tribus, that they should go together, surprised and captivated him.

They could lie under the last trees before the desert began, and watch the slow caresses of the sand at the roots of the grass frontier. The women of les tribus were painting the silk they wore – bars of feather-shapes, blocks of black, red, green, silver, spreading out in wedges – while the lynxes snapped at their chains, and the men shouted to each other, as they circled the flocks endlessly on furry red-gold horses.

‘The magic apple tree,’ said Curzon, staring up through the branches.

‘I’m sorry about the lynxes,’ said Shala.

‘It’s a pity,’ said Osman, ‘that one needs a multiple consciousness but has only one simple, if dense, layer. You were telling us how you slipped through Europe – a remembered landscape, a landscape of remembrance – taking in impressions in a series of incredulous blinks. Here the writing on a bill, there a headline, there some words of a reflected chocolate advertisement, and always conversations remembered word for word and strained through this fine mesh of your unchangeable monist consciousness. So the crossed wires, the capillary and fragmented scraps of information, twisted out of the general to-and-fro swash of nothing – tortured, as it were, from and even in to your own swing-door mind – all end on the ever-absorbent blotting paper inside your head.'

The hawks circled over the city like the balls of soot and ashes which circled every city after Tienen. 'In every bottle of wine,' said Curzon, producing one, 'lies a crumb of the central agate, and a reel of the same interminable film. But so what? The tension between desert and lemon trees, between les tribus and the classes of the city – this volatile frontier is what must concern us – not the tie-rods and rivets in my head. The wine does not make things clearer – it speeds up the accumulation of experiences, and in time increases the incidence of "white spots" in the mental sequence, encourages the elision of cause and effect, so that there are only causes and at times only effects. Not only are the elisions more frequent, but we can hop sideways from one heap of cultural rubble to the next faster – but that is all.'

They were both satisfied with the shape of their argument. Two men making astrakhan caps also reached agreement. 'I will forget your caste so long as we have to work together in this stinking-gut palace,' said one. 'And I, for the time being, will ignore your accent,' said the other, 'but if you think that makes us a unit of industrial warfare, you're a sheep yourself.'

Prompted by Curzon, Shala brought in one day one of the Russian documents les tribus were now collecting in the hope they had political significance.

'*Russia under the tsars!*' said the page of the diary, in a young girl's handwriting.

All summer I have sat on the terrace, watching Nikon the idiot balancing on his barrel along the alleys of lime-trees. The lilac in the moonlight looks as white as our tablecloths. Alexei has a beard which hardly moves when he smiles at me – I think that is frightening, even unbecoming. We shall ride into the village – but the peasants must make no ceremony. I am seventeen, when Gregory returns from Petersburg, shall I come down to the terrace in the moonlight? Shall I give myself in the moonlight, under the lilacs, in the sticky-sweet that the lime trees have dropped, in the alley of lime trees, where poor Nikon stands on his barrel and crows and flaps his arms. No, I must not think of it – for Nikon would cry if I went away, if I gave myself like a peasant girl under the lime trees – and I should never again see Papa's servants, and the telescope he bought in Kazan. If I go away with Gregor – dear God, but the scent of the lime trees tears at me – they will laugh about me in the village. Today, poor Nikon gave me a stick he had carved – he is so gentle, and I am afraid of Alexei's smile. But I can't tell Nikon anything – he would feel I would be hurt by Gregor, and I am, I am.

Russia under the tsars! Why can nothing change this, why will these lime trees, this lilac burning purple by day and silver by night, never change? Will the snow cool this torment? This summer will burn me, until I have the look of a peasant girl. Will I be able then to go with him under the lime trees? Will he come back from Peterburg?

Shala smiled at him when he finished his translating. ‘Perhaps the peasants came for her, in the end. Poor Nikon. The summer burning away so fiercely, and the lime trees like candlesticks burning with wax made of animal fat and roses – and the girl in the white blouse, pouring out tea, asking if rye bread was bad for the skin, burning away from the centre. Perhaps she was entirely consumed and in the end only wanted Gregor to lead the peasants to their death, fighting each other – displacing her torment on those who raked the gravel and washed the tablecloths.’

‘Yes, these are all snapshots through the keyhole – one finds only scenes so haphazard, so often in any case obscured by armchairs, servants poking the fire and so forth, that only the fact that they are images on one’s own cerebral celluloid makes them memorable. Indeed, it makes them the only things one can remember. But I think you’re hard on the girl.’

‘There are millions of letters dumped in the sand, to say nothing of libraries, a score of cities with the remains of the drainage systems for a hundred more – we of les tribus cannot take too seriously the possibility of a few wrong judgments. She’s lucky to win any comment at all: and luckier still than Nikon. It is, after all, as if this girl, with her one known action, had pulled the trigger of a rifle which fired through time – and winged both of us. To be fair, then, I should say we know she had bequeathed two actions – the writing of the diary and the transmission to us—’

‘But this is all thin stuff. Isn’t it enough to say that each of these growth rings sees and comments on every other? Usually with invective, memoranda, graffiti, private and universal jokes, nudges, cracker mottos, 'Redfront' biscuit wrappers – very much like those dumps in the desert of correspondence, request, complaints, condolence.'

That seemed to sum it up. As they sat together on the roof of the observatory they could see the lines of animals queuing outside the slaughterhouse to have their throats cut and their forelegs broken.

'Should we play the pebble game?' asked Shala.

'Why not.'

But Curzon was aware that as he watched Shala smoothly following the rules of the pebble game, the impulse to break the rules on his own master game became intense. Even though he knew that the only links between himself and the couriers could be political and administrative, he knew too that the obstinately single layer of consciousness he was equipped with was carried off, bound by all four imaginary limbs, by Shala, and by 'the pebble game and Shala'.

Sadik had always claimed that to withhold love from Shala was not only pointless, but also made a mockery of the imminent revolution which, Curzon hoped, would expedite and deepen this kind of relationship. Osman, on the other hand, believed Curzon's sensibility was forever deficient – and such was Curzon's sensibility that he indeed understood Osman's unexpressed valuation, and agreed with it.

This would be fine, thought Curzon, were I in love with Osman. But for the moment, let me just think of ways of combining café groups with the groups in the tea houses.

'The only thing I possess is my creativity – I don't own my life,' said Osman. 'You, Curzon, are not really concerned that you will lose your life before you have lived it out to the full –

you are afraid that when you die you will not have scratched the surface of your existence, not even untied the string. As for hurting other people, I have to take something of a chance. But at least, if I am misguided in resisting with force, I do not base my whole argument on my own deficiencies, as you do. In recognising the logic of my own position, I try to demonstrate this logic to as many as possible, and to convince them that they will not buy their emancipation by killing me. I certainly do not believe that my hope of emancipation lies in killing others.'

Cuzon and Osman spent the days in the lemon groves now occupied by les tribus, the evenings with Sadik discussing with the others from the literal the direction of their movement. At times a star would swim around until it struck one of the sights of the observatory, covered now with thin membranes, and lit up the underground chamber. The couriers called the stars after the effect of light they produced – the tiger, blue sword – and seemed to listen only for the noise the stork made in its nest on the copola of the observatory.

But Shala once interrupted one of the 'Friends of Otto Bauer' when he remarked 'Now we are living under "tiger", soon under "blue sword" or "blue fish"; but this is nonsense, for as soon as we leave the observatory the effect is gone – and like as not we should be arrested, or whatever. Were the observatory as large as the city, then we could predict, we could have a universal and acclaimed success. But until then…'

'We couriers know which stars strike out which light when we are in the open,' said Shala, 'and in any case in the desert we are not concerned with the stability of the observatory, but the movement of the lights. It seems to me that the "Friends of Otto Bauer" want to lie still under the stars, and blame les tribus for inventing names for what happens when their light strikes the parchments on those holes in the roof. We couriers are not magicians, but neither are we afraid of the books in the silted libraries. Our strength is that we have none of the crippling nostalgia of the "Friends" – just as we have no doubts about the efficacy of our culture – as Curzon does about his.

'We have two layers in our language – one layer of words which do not reproduce themselves, an old language never written down, and of whose syntax we are quite ignorant, and the other a layer of words which act as roots so that we can continue to describe what changes about us. This means a great many objects and people have words found in both languages to describe them – but we don't feel we are using dead words. We simply use them in parallel: it is a test of skill and sensibility to use them with delicacy and harmony – but we all know the double language. And you must realise that it is from les tribus that there can most easily come a revolution, because you do not have to create in les tribus the relationships, the intuitive connections, which have to be rediscovered or invented in your city movement …'

Sadik felt uncomfortable during these discussions. He felt in Shala's complaints at the conventions he tried to follow in organising a political party a tendency towards a purely anecdotal and analogical politics. He had seen in Elizabeth what he took to be the source of Curzon's constraint and his fear of emotional atrophy. He worried all the time Osman and

Curzon were together, chasing foxes away from the groves of fruit trees, composing ghazals, because he believed they could both hide in a secret inner bolthole, where they would be able to resist the purely physical pains which he dreaded.

After the other had slipped back to the city, Curzon would sit with Sadik, Osman and Shala talking in most of the languages under the sand. 'Les tribus have very few objects to label: indeed, the townsmen too get by with a few dozen words for animals, buildings, trees, minerals and so on. We describe emotions either by analogy with these objects, or by using terms from other languages. At the same time, the processes which exist have a huge vocabulary: every stage of a race between lynxes, for instance, has minute differentiations and distinctions – and their correct use is half the fun of the racing,' said Shala.

'But we surely are not to imagine that your political contribution will be in terms of philology? These are all pleasant ideas you are giving us, but all irrelevant – even to yourselves,' said Sadik.

'I just want to convince Curzon that les tribus have a complexity and sensibility which will allow them to deal with any appeal the urban movement may make – heavily simplified. I don't for a moment believe that our language divides us from our neighbours – only that it helps us in particular ways to perceive processes, even though we've only a small supply of different kinds of objects in the desert.'

The conscripts walked hand in hand about the sandy squares, and giggled when their officers approached. Young lieutenants in limousines would lead the stronger infantrymen to manoeuvres in the desert, allowing them to take one bucket of water for every ten men. And after a few days three or four survivors would crawl back to be court-martialled and shot for desertion. But many conscripts believed the army was preferable to five years at a university – which they could not afford. If they ran away from university they were arrested for fraudulent use of government property and sent to complete their five years' education on those estates where serfdom had recently been abolished by decree.

Some merchants called a meeting to protest at the system of conscription and education. 'The need of our youth for an outlet for its idealism and "service before everything", as Tolstoy said, can best be met by service in the mines. Then we can send home the foreigners who work the mines and debauch our women. After five years in the mines, it should be easy to see who has any idealism left – and those we can control better with the police than an expensive army of conscripts. In the desert, you understand me, they are not under the eyes of their officers – besides, they may abscond to les tribus.'

Another man proposed that there should be no difference between conscription to the university and to the army: only convention at present separated the terms.

'The university contains the whole of life and the whole of life is guaranteed by the counter-insurgency programme of the army. There is no contradiction here, and for the sake of our boys in the desert, I believe it is disloyal to hold otherwise. Besides, the fusion of university and army means that Americans can at the same time support both our institutions for promoting and enforcing variety of opinion – and punishing any form of military disobedience or any lapse from academic standards.'

A third suggested that in place of an army there should be a regional militia, trained in the universities for counter-insurgency, and paid according to the amount of insurgency they discovered.

'Surely you realise this is already planned,' said another. 'And that in any case to leave such things to amateurs and universities is counter-productive. The quieter these activities are kept, the more separate we keep institutions, the harder it becomes for any radical to find his comrades, and to start a group of any wider significance and deep penetration. In the last resort we, as guardians of ideology and of property, have only to be calm and sensible. It is bad business for the nation if people starve: I don't pay taxes so that people should nonetheless die of neglect. Our enemy is disruption – not a dole.'

However, all those who spoke were sternly questioned by the police, and were forced to pay heavily to remove their names from a list of political suspects.

'I am lost to my parents,' a little girl told the policemen.

'Lost, or lost to?' he asked. Every day people had taken to reporting themselves lost, abandoned, or in some form of truncated relationship with their family, their work, their class. The religious authorities had forbidden all forms of self-denial, unselfishness and meditation, so that the harvest could be gathered, inflation controlled, and the sale of food continued. The beggars were joined by rich merchants, starving from very love of starvation, discovering, before they flew off to recover in sanatoria, a keen delight in misery and humiliation. The newspapers acclaimed 'a new children's pilgrimage', and some even proposed landing those who proclaimed themselves lost in the battle zones of the world.

In the city's governing bodies proposals for more varied military service were discussed, with deportation as an alternative. One deputy would claim, 'My son has reported himself lost, and speaks only "old language" to the police. My daughter tells me the only way to break through the crust we have baked over her at such expense is to gallop about naked on a red horse.' He laughed. 'Where would we find a red horse?'

Such popular delusions and fashions appeared and spread – until in the streets there were daily passwords: paramilitary organisations multiplied, 'generals' carrying branches of frangipani jostled the workers on the sidewalks, and broke up union meetings. Some of these organisations took a religious form and religious wars were fought out in the cinemas between 'buddhists' and 'transcendentalists': peace-workers formed their own societies.

The initial phase of decadence in the arts was replaced by even more feverish creation, institutionalised decadence – some artists even proposed that they should be ripped up by crowds themselves. Sentimental and exotic work attracted much attention – but little was sold. The owners of cinemas and taxi-dance halls were able to buy out the bands of paladins who sold them protection. Men and women began to dress like the people of les tribus. It was as if a tinselly utopia had transformed the shops and offices of the city into a haven of dreary simplicity for les tribus, but les tribus hated the patronage implicit in this; they found their urban derivatives unsophisticated, unhelpful and contemptuous.

'What they like about us is our docility, our poverty, our insecurity – these things we need their help to fight. But our customs, the naming of processes, the making of distinctions – this they confuse with our poverty,' said Shala. 'They picture us as dead things, our clothes as fancy dress; they deny their own reality by adopting some surface elements of ours. Where I want to build socialism, they think I must abolish myself, and destroy my sensibility. I think when the time comes, les tribus of the desert fringe will confront with hostility les tribus of the airline offices and the taxi-dance.'

And what if I love Shala, thought Curzon. Since I translate what she says, am I half in love with my own turns of phrase, mistranslations? But then, if she loved me, it could not be her translations she loved – and surely I'm not so clogged with verbal apprehensions I can't trust myself? And yet, the silence before making a decisive gesture is so peaceful and profound – before the jeering, the pounding of feet from the audience breaks out again – perhaps the audience is really watching something quite other? And yet, how foolish, for indecisiveness considers and embraces all sorts of unlikely actions, it has its own seductiveness. And if I said there could be no revolution if I stayed with Elizabeth, no one could doubt that Shala would not see it delayed a minute.

Curzon had a letter wheedled through to him from Elizabeth: racked with tender incomprehension, that nostalgia, that calculated awareness, it made him long to share that profoundly competent ignorance which Elizabeth produced so easily. She melted into her surroundings so easily that she became surroundings: to renounce Elizabeth was like renouncing an earth and a sky. Was she infinitely subtle, infinitely adaptable – or just an excellent conductor to whom sewage, electricity, made neither more nor less demands on her natural permeability – product of bourgeois manufactories, designed for England, but equally functional everywhere.

She talked about new furniture, jokes her dog had made, new kinds of food – teasing away at Curzon's memory, endlessly, falsely naïve, always successful. It was impossible to say if this was a perfect design or a perfect functioning: only at the end did she again, by implication, suggest that he might lavish on her still a love she could not enjoy – for reasons of taste – a love she did not care to renounce since it was a measure of her understanding of his needs and failings.

'What can she want for herself?' asked Curzon. 'She leaves me because of my failings – yet they are failings which should stop her interest in me, since my only desirable quality is my persistence. Perhaps she felt a responsibility to me once, and this has curdled into sentiment, but clearly she cannot develop her own selfishness and weakness, since she does not trust me. She is submitting to intolerable tension only in the hope that she will break, and that this collapse will transform us into someone she is compelled, from very prostration, to like. I think silence is the best solution. It includes decision, and indecision, as well as postal misdirection.'

'I find in here a paradigm of the state,' said the prison governor, hopping on one leg like a stork the length of his study. 'We have made the prisoners lay out an exercise yard in black and white marble squares. Black and white on the walls.

But on the slabs we found centipedes, gestures in tar. This forever chaste and forever deceptive progression of receding squares was always spoiled by the rubbish the prisoners left, the problems of maintenance which meant we had to replace marked white tiles with black, In a purely formal, minimally coercive legal system, we found the prisoners had not only to be accommodated – they took a positive delight in damaging our formalism.

'And so I hated them so much that I keep them out of the exercise yard altogether – and the prison is model indeed. What a magnificent background! what indeterminate relationships, what games of speculative remembrance, can be played out on these squares. I can ponder all day over an imagined comma in my memoirs, over a possible fold in a tea-gown, the precise degree of invitation in an almost forgotten smile by a woman recollected by way of a thousand others, always revisiting and re-smiling, always new and archaic, dreamlike but never dreamt, real as the stuff in my head, but existing only separate from it …' Hop, hop: his dress sword jutted out like a bird's tail.

He gobbled some tokay grapes, dusty and blue. Some prisoners were watching a puppet show, performed by angular, flat, metal dancers. They could hear the rattle of billiard balls from the tables in the converted mosque against the prison walls, and the noises of geese in the reservoir, tric-trac, and the soft, knowing laughter of les tribus in the tea-house.

'When I was a young man,' said the governor, 'there was nothing I'd not do for people. I used to bury bones for my dog in the garden, and rise at midnight to dig them up again. But then I trained in the law, and fell in love. But where I succeeded in law, I failed with the girl – and my jealousies forced me to order my memories as comprehensively as I could. Striving for that chastity of memory and expression, I had also to keep the paths to the past open, clean – and to lay fresh ones. And always there was vegetable waste around, leaves blowing over the wall, prisoners spitting and so forth. I tried to feed all this into my early memories of empire: ladies in fur coming to watch we cadets play class-war games, the locked doors and gingerbread surprises in the summer residence, the words the grooms taught us which killed Mama. But of course, it was impossible.

'Had I entered the colonial service,' he added wistfully, 'we could have talked to important men – men selling bathroom fittings, police inspectors – and walked to and fro in white. White, and our epaulettes painted black in mourning – or in black, with white epaulettes: I forget.'

He was silent for some time, and the prisoner began to cheer up.

But the governor shouted, 'And that is why I hate you. Remember that every kindness, every gesture of decency you have here, is given because I have no choice. I have orders which compel me to be kind to you, I have preoccupations which make me absent-minded and benevolent, but basically I can only tolerate other prison governors. Here within these walls, I am only interested in the morphology of my memory. You're not brilliant, are you? Then I won't help you. You're not a gentleman either, so I'll not employ you in the prison.'

He turned his back, and the prisoner thought sadly about the ice cream he could be eating in the park, the dogs and little children he could be patting …

'I only put up a poster,' he pleaded. 'It said, "Capitalists are not immortal, whatever their laws may suggest." I promise you, it and my action were as inept as they sound.'

'Why should I care? You're a no-account person. You're easy to catch because you're stupid – do you propose we shouldn't catch you? I suppose you want us to concentrate on the clever ones! Where would we be then?'

'I can tell you where an agitator, an Englishman, is hiding.'

'Nonsense. Stupid. You've even been caught by our propaganda. All answers lie in the shifting planes of memory. Or at least, the one answer I want lies there.'

'To hell with you then. I'll joggle up your memory myself.'

However, there was capillary heroism. Austere and incommunicable trials of strength took place between the police and defecting informers, police spies and spies on the point of mutiny. Men arrested for minor political offences – incautious conversation, chalking, dropping leaflets – began to defend themselves and principles which seemed to come to them by intuition, where previously they would have sworn innocence. Sabotage which might be carelessness, and carelessness which had the effect of sabotage, affected the supplies for the troops. Men in the arms factory talked to each other in a lapsed demotic not understood by their foremen. As irony and self-awareness increased, so did desertions from the army.

'Yes,' Sadik wondered, 'have we lost control of the movement?'

'We were never in control – that is for governments. We have now reached the point where the old structures are looking shabby – and conforming more nearly to what we have always said was their inner quality. We shall now see if they can manage to defend and even perpetuate themselves. Perhaps they will crumble like mushrooms, loosing off clouds of dead spores. Perhaps they'll kill us with a touch. But they are stripped of their deceptions. The army is ready to fire on the peasants, the police have kicked aside the laws, the better to get to grips with us. And yet, it seems to me, there were never such roses as this year – and they never made such jam from them ...' Osman smiled round at them all. He lay in his position of pretended abandon – as if to say, 'Whatever happens, I can enjoy myself. My roof needs no stork.'

Curzon said, 'If one is in love, the question of control, *dirigisme*, looks rather different. Is one in control of one's pottering around the familiar contours of one's affections? Let alone when the tigers come, and it's sweet murder for everyone.'

And Shala said, 'Who brings love into it all? Who' (half mocking, half asking) 'is this Curzon who grows up from Otto Bauer in a few weeks, and rattles away about love in the middle of his own hunting down by the most cruel and most diffuse police and military service in Asia? Who is he, Osman?'

Elizabeth's letter whispered in his pocket. 'The dogs are well. I am in the Bach choir again. My blue dress is too daring, so I'll not wear it until you are near, my love, my darling.

Please do not kill anyone, for you know you can't believe in this …'

And Osman replied, 'Curzon is a big man, tucked away inside a little one. Who cares that he reach his full stature? Yes, I do for one. We're not so splendid we can let our chief theorist stay a dwarf …'

Under the lime trees, thought Curzon, where we would have our books, there is always a double line of policemen. Wherever we rush to meet each other, there are posters defaced by our couriers, in every police barracks our names lies in sealed envelopes, ready for the day when, after all our indeterminate arguments we take the action we must … Osman is right – that I have to come to terms with what I want, and Shala is right, that my identity depends on how I approach her. Let me only say that if we must kill our enemies, I want to be the first of us to go…'

A few days later, Osman proposed that the city's students should hold a demonstration. 'I've thought of it: Sadik can organise it, and Curzon rationalise it. We'll be able to see how it goes from the observatory.'

'Well,' said Sadik,'the students are certainly a soft edge of any insurrection. And who can tell but that we may find a few useful people emerging from this?'

But Shala was irritated by 'This habit of organising sections of protest. It is on les tribus that the main burdens will fall – why pretend otherwise to the students? Why should they have their own little street battles, why should they be told that because they can't pass their exams they should become a political vanguard? These people are the least likely to make a serious contribution to the movement as it is growing, and the most likely to demand privileges when it has succeeded.

'The men of les tribus are already coming to the lemon groves armed. A group of bagpipers and dancers arrived the other day and started to satirise the peasants, and for once the townspeople did not stand there laughing. You keep looking at the police, the police informers, the students, the newspapers, and so you never see that you are communicating with les tribus. The old frontiers are beginning to collapse – and yet you seem to be building them again.

'The best things that happen in a student demonstration are that Osman composes a ghazal, and that Curzon talks to me about the apricot trees, the mud cupolas, the silver and dun goats that he can see from the observatory. But apart from some droplets of self-knowledge, the whole exercise is useless.'

'But no – as an exercise, it has its uses,' said Sadik, 'because we can't bring les tribus into town now. Better to have the students demonstrating than the unions.'

'I don't see why. "My feet sink into the sand,"' she quoted, '"but the sand stops them breaking through the roofs of tombs."'

Sadik said that this sounded unremarkable enough, and that in any case, he proposed to bring in the unions in force only when there was no danger of them losing momentum too early, developing a conciliatory mood.

Curzon thought only of his own cultural dislocation, and of the Russian girl, whose diary had continued,

And now we have a Russia under the soviets, and I have seen for the first time the eyes of people I thought were dead – the gardeners, the grooms, their sons racing back from the front to take our land, to take the canvas awning where I sit with Sonia to do lessons, and to take me down the alleys of lime trees, to take me, and their eyes are burning, and no one comes from Peterburg. To take me under the lilac trees – and the gardeners have not even picked up the watering can they left there a week ago … and I shall never be able to order them. And I shall belong to them. But what will they do to me? And the scent of the lilac has driven me mad, and will no one ever come from Peterburg? Why is the dew so heavy this year? And the lilac so sweet?

And when the students demonstrated, it was all as Shala had said. But those in the observatory thought Osman's ghazal exceptional this time.

'How about this as a start, "Steady! We have not fled, we are not beaten, and even should they throw us in chains, we are there, and shall remain" – even though it has been used before.'

'You feel we're condemned to be Spartacists, then?' asked Shala. She had once more urged Curzon to join her and operate with les tribus, and he once more had insisted that only success in the town signified.

'I'm not only thinking of what you will find politically, but of what needs doing to you. As things are, you're sweet and ingenious. Your mind is like an immense mechanical game, made to intrigue and exasperate: it's like a great toy city, made for rats – full of surprise sewers and traps, here a granary, there a miniature coal-hopper to be filled from the nursery scuttle. From a fund of sensibility you throw out whimsy, obduracy, isolation and volubility – but the complete person is not there.

'It's rather as if you had not been joined up: here are exquisite nerve endings putting out signals in all known, and three or four unknown, languages – but what is the brain sending or receiving them? Are there several brains? At this stage we need a multiple intelligence, but when we succeed it will be a liability. What use will your concern with Elizabeth's air-blue clothes, her dogged sexual obsession whose aim was to encircle and dominate you completely – what use will this be when we need you to take your place in a success?

'I know you are trying to explain how a revolution can be made with the aid of all kinds of social cripples like yourself, how the wretched of the earth will rise up in awareness of their wretchedness to make a society in which their actions and experiences would be unthinkable, unnecessary. But you do not want to be like them, surely? Such a revolution won't strip off your carapace, won't test your seams, tighten your connections…'

'Perhaps I should come down off this catwalk if I'm such a shambling albatross to you all.'

'You see! You even idealise your infirmity. You've come to believe people should love you because you're deficient.'

And yet don't I, she wondered, or is all this a ploy, to make me take notice?

'I may just simulate all this,' said Curzon, 'to make myself look pale and interesting.'

But, he thought, since she doesn't like me, there would not be much point in that.

They were sitting high in the rood of the observatory, near the point where the sextant, like a moon's horn, pierced the cupola. They were peeling fruit with three skins – silver, purple, green – and a composite nucleus of multi-coloured seeds, and miniature nuts.

Shala said, 'I met a woman today who said, "I always treated my husband with the bathos I thought amused him. Yesterday I found a letter he was writing to our daughter – granitic, scornful: 'silly cheerful bitch', he called me. And now I'm destroyed – the manner has taken me over completely." And she stood there trying to teach me about both of us … I have no intention of that happening to me.'

Yes, then, I must go to les tribus, thought Curzon. But in a few days.

In the honeycombing under the cupola, there clung colonies of nocturnal animals. There were moths a foot across, scratched and foxy like old parchment, with shiny black eyes. Things like kittens hung upside-down and mewed. Creatures resembling furry woodlice pottered slowly up the wall, and then swished, half jumping, half flying, to some lower point.

When the light of a star swung round to them, they hunched away, or continued hobbling about as if almost ashamed of the smallness of their range and of the world they had chosen to explore. At times you could hear the delicate crackle of bones as the stranger encountered a weaker body fumbling its way past them, and decided, in a speculative way, to gobble it up. Ribbons of cold flesh which had not quite become lizard, but was clearly not intended to be worm, fringed every smooth surface. Only in the persistence of their clinging did they seem adapted to the changes which Curzon and Sadik bought to their environment.

Sadik hated the climb to the top of the sextant, from which they could peer out through cracks in the clay tiles at the dusty trees and the massive clay walls of the city. 'It's silly to be frightened of things which have so few feelings and such little sense of direction. Perhaps they remind me of prisoners – and this is silly, for my uncle was in prison.'

'Where?' asked Curzon.

'In Russia, after the revolution – long after. So naturally, I'm more wary of my own efforts.'

Only in the evenings could they see signs of marked increases in activity – the fires in the soldiers' field-kitchens, groups of peasants squatting round naphtha flares, singing and drinking, tea-houses humming with ill-suppressed radicalism so distracting that the tric-trac players protested. In the more distant suburbs, men met in the dark, or at street corners, talking of their present lives as if these were of no further interest or value, something to be shed like rough dead skin.

'Might I enquire, how red is your tie?' asked a police informer.

'If I'd my way, we'd abolish the working class: nasty, brutish, and short. That's how I'd describe them, my dear,' said the professor.

'We're not animals,' protested a girl in the cavalry's brothel.

'We'll see about that,' was the promise.

At the writers' circle, a motion deprecating decadence was rushed through.

'I think there's a lot to be said to be said within decadence,' said Osman.

'That's because you're one of those who wants to spread defeatism,' said Sadik.

'On the contrary, I want to be the first to bring news of defeat.'

In the fields, the peasants worked guarded by soldiers: a peasant thought, 'Perhaps this will be our last harvest. Perhaps the king of the peasants will come and establish his heaven right here – then we'll have meat every week, and new clothes each year.'

'You're mad if you think that will ever be,' said a soldier. 'Who do you think you are. What right have you to be happy? Even a soldier doesn't have that, and he's got the gun, so what are you talking about? In our village, if the men wanted meat every week, we should know they were off to steal: "never trust a hungry bandit," we say. Do you say that?'

But the peasant was silent.

'A tenderness shared is a tenderness halved,' said Curzon.

'Am I so tough, then?' asked Shala. 'It's good you can have such gentleness and be so patient, when we're so vulnerable, when we've such little time. At first I thought your response was just feeble, but now I think it is of a subtlety to outlast even Osman's.

'When I was small, I would sit on the cart and ride scratching out a poem on a clay brick, or whatever, or my uncles would teach me to read some new script. Our carts were lined with hay, with a little tent of bark or leather so that my father could lie flat and go to sleep after pointing the mule in the right direction. I never thought then that the good opinion of an English would matter to me …'

'And yet, so many things should be talked over, while for us there is no time. I agree that you should not want me to tip every reminiscence from the folds of my mind, but there must be some process of exchange. I'm not granitic, not expository.'

'Perhaps if we were together among les tribus …'

In their state of permanent tension, the smallest errand became a potential martyrdom: they knew many who had to report every day to the police – then every hour, until they lived as beggars on the steps of the police station, charged with nothing, wholly circumscribed by the precise adherence to legal forms. Every time Shala worked as a courier, she thought only of speeches of defiance, whilst every leaf, each bowl of apricots, each spiral of cooking smoke from the shacks beneath the walls, had the pungency and the force of childhood.

'Since I am to die anyway, let me revel in the name of revolutionary. If I am a terrorist, it is to terrorise those who practise savagery and exploitation. If my efforts to transform the hardship and injustice which les tribus have always met mean I have to die, then I am only glad that they should be noticed, and my punishment becomes a mark of your despair. So long as I am alive, I testify to your failure, and in the moment of my death I testify to your brutality and fear …' Every day Shala passed notionally through the courts and before the firing squad a dozen times.

'Will the comrade give me a light please?' asked the man she had bumped into.

'That's an odd way to address a girl,' she said, frightened and curious.

'Yours must be a mouth bitter with sorrel, that you take exception to that. "Let us make a rope from the joining of our hands, and let it reach from here to the Soviets" – as they used to say long ago. My grandfather told me it would come, that the town must join with les tribus before we could be comrades.'

'What do you do?'

'Railways. Track maintenance.'

'Are there many who think like you?'

'You're out of date. But the men from les tribus are better than I could ever be. They talk to us when we're mending the track. Or they used to, before they put a police guard on us.'

'What happened to the men from les tribus?'

'Chased away. A few shot. You should go back.'

High conjecture indeed – and Shala felt a longing to be back with les tribus, for all that the man had called her comrade.

A man a long way away was singing a song, full of glottal hesitations, little hopping, limping syllables – 'sh'sh, sh'chch', and Shala thought of Curzon's quotation, 'Spartacus crushed? … Steady, we have not fled, we are not beaten …' and the voice fading and distorting came back, 'Sh'sh, ch'sh …

It was the beginning of autumn: here and there a tree had turned a bright red, acting as a kind of vanguard to the other dusty and dun shrubs. The camions of the police crushed the berries on the stalk as they rattled through the forest fringe. For the children, war games predominated. Bandits began offering their services to the army.

The bride prices among the peasants fell since all anticipated that daughters would soon return as widows to their fathers' families. Everyone agreed that any brief social convulsion would be preferable to a long eroding crisis. Sadik spent his days watching police headquarters through a telescope, and the police themselves began to build detention camps, and ordered parkas against a winter campaign.

In the capital, the prime minister summoned the British ambassador: they swam side by side, in the warm, scented water of the swimming pool, the prime minister's tall black turban held carefully aloft like a funnel as he performed an expressive breast-stroke.

'See here, Cunninghame. I've nothing against you personally: you come here and swim about, and I don't worry about where you've been, what you've done lately. You're my guest, and any personal habits of yours I may or may not have heard about – that's your affair. There's good and bad in any country. But one of your Englishmen is up in the provinces making trouble, and quite frankly if I can't get rid of him, I'd as soon get rid of you. It's your job to cancel him out – I've enough of my own lot who need the short answer and the long rope. In my young days, they'd tie a man up so, dragging him along, going their own ways, or whatever. We'd put burrs as big as sea-urchins under their saddles, so even the horses didn't enjoy it much … Swell notion, huh?'

'Her Britannic Majesty's government can have no official opinion on such matters – and for myself I'm not in the least concerned with your horsy tricks. As you know, I find you personally uncongenial: I have in any case thought that garrotting was a dramatic and humane method. Horses! Let the lynxes run till they burst, I say – and you think I should be dismayed by insults and nonsense about Englishmen! I suggest that any corpse you may find with an English passport must have stolen or forged it.'

'So there's a soft centre to your rudeness? – excellent. Let's get out, and I'll have the water changed.'

They went, incautiously, to see a film about a tiny American, caught 'on the West Virginia line'.

Sadik thought unconcernedly, 'Will they use dogs on us?' and was caught by a passionate attack of fear.

Today we went to Nelepograd, so that our guardian might look into our affairs and listen to our aspirations. When we got home, the gardeners had left bowls of sour cherries for us. We could see their carts raising the yellow dust over the yellow sheaves. Timofei's little grandson came up to us, bearing a magnificent sheaf – so heavy and furry that it pushed him over: goodness, how he cried! We talked about the management of the estate till it was dark, and nightingales came into the garden. But when the others had gone to bed, you could hear singing from the village. What would they do if I went down to them, away from this scent of lilac which is burning me away? Would the men of the estate send me home? Or would their eyes burn when they saw me? Will this summer never end? Why won't the lilac fade…?

In her letter, Elizabeth had said, ‘I do so admire what you are doing – but remember that it must come to an end, and at that end I will be waiting for you. Today on the bus a man stared at me in such a nasty way – he was quite young and good-looking too. I wish you were here to save me from all that sort of thing. I’m sorry, that makes me sound very helpless, but you know what I mean …’

‘What are the winters like here?’ Curzon asked Shala.

‘If I describe it to you, it will sound as if les tribus spend months commenting on the various aspects of cold amber suns in the green sky. But really, there is not much to do. The food has mostly been preserved from the summer, and people talk about what they did then while they are eating: there is a cycle of winter dances, “Down goes the sun”, “Did I love a concept”, “In the next river there are fine lilies”, and “The shoes of the general’s horse are made of silver.” But no one likes these very much. Those of us who enjoy sifting the sands for books do that. The others often fight.’

‘It seems to me that this is mere subsistence. I don’t see how you can be well-rounded in the sense that you and I understood when so much of your life derives from poverty and prohibition.’

‘Well, you must come and see,’ said Shala. ‘I believe myself that our customs are more fluid and creative than most, that they are not a derivative of poverty, but imaginative leaps beyond it. When I ask you to come to les tribus I do not propose you accept things because there is no alternative: but just that our participation will be more close to socialism than the populism of the towns, so deeply coloured by yesterday’s ideas, forgotten empires of former ruling classes.’

And Curzon was nearer than ever in his conviction, if only because Shala was looking at him without fear, and with that air of saying, 'Nothing you do or say can disturb my good opinion of you – because I know you could never fail to consider my feelings, knowing each other as we do…'

'There must in this be some evidence of a conflict of good with good,' said Curzon. 'But in general I can't see sober and honest citizens arming to defend themselves against us. On the contrary, the army and the police seem virtually detached from those they claim to serve – they are aggressive where the others are passive, unpredictable and vicious, where townsmen are riveted to custom.'

Shala was becoming impatient with their campaign in the town. Once when Curzon asked her what she would do afterwards she told him angrily that there was no such time, and because of the delays their chance of exerting any pressure on the movement was slipping away:

'Some people fritter away their own lives, but develop sufficient charm to persuade others to share their impotence.'

'Yes, surely,' replied Curzon, 'just as they prefer to avoid pain rather than take the chance of giving pleasure. I suppose that is a classic system of self-absorption.'

'Les tribus used to own land: only by dispossession, by becoming so poor that bandits did not trouble us, by losing the ability to pay bride prices and so on, did we win independence from the old carousel of abductions, patriarchy. But before we could think of acting as a political force, we had to suffer the breaking of our old customs – and by finding new ones understand something of social and cultural processes. For les tribus in their poverty, it has been not “who/whom” but “we/us”.

‘We have had to work hard not to suffer – and to me the avoidance of misery requires action and participation. You think you can avoid having a relationship of any depth with me because to do so would be difficult and dangerous personally and politically. But this refusal itself presupposes a high degree of intimacy, while it also implies a contempt and coldness towards me, a disregard for me which reflects on your politics. Your kindness becomes tainted with passivity, your good sense with indolence and despair.’

‘I can see Osman playing tric-trac. Sadik is looking for places to paint slogans. You have made me ashamed, my dear Shala. I seem only to live inside my own head. Do you remember that section of the diary –

> *The dust from the threshing is rising so high that it melts into the sun. We can smell the dust, the sweat of the horses, crushed berries, the fresh mousy smell of the grain. And the lilac burns like candles. I have to give myself to the peasants …*

‘And suppose she had done – in the avenue of limes, to anyone who wanted – that delicate severe girl, with her Peterburg fashions … What cruelty, what pleasure and seriousness, for the peasants of the estate – and for her what a revenge, if she should wish it: at once fulfilment, torment, an act of total social and political submission springing from that bitter summer and its bitter lust.’

‘I cannot argue with you. I can only say that in waiting for emancipation you may find the flesh has absorbed the metal of the fetters: unless you take care, you will find that political emancipation will not release you from yourself.'

The last lizards scuttled like leaves into cracks in the city's clay fortifications. Osman felt that at least he could write down his ghazal – guiltily, for it was not concerned with the dialectic, but with the acrid women of the ports. It amused him that his choice of a relatively strict and traditional form should contrast so sharply with his material, which dealt with the modes of remembrance, and his political activity. Yet there was even in such a form the chances of transcending ordinary nastiness and common boredom.

'I must be irretrievably minor,' thought Osman, 'but at least it's not for want of choice of styles and forms. Whatever I say I can, notionally, say in half a dozen dialects, hybrid language, court slang and so on. But the perfection of a dying form presents its own challenges, petty though the exercise may be.'

He thought of Curzon and Shala – Curzon's obstinacy growing gigantically, forever ingeniously devising reasons for denying his own humanity, and Shala's obsession that the last months of her life should not be subordinated to practical considerations. Osman suspected that the customs of lynx racing, kite-flying, had been instituted by Shala a few weeks before the revolutionaries had arrived in the city, and that she would have gone on to devise fresh customs when these became tedious.

At times he thought that between Curzon and Shala there could only be some deathbed reconciliation in which the poignancy and wistfulness would linger on only as a kind of catalogue of missed opportunities. There was beginning to be a danger that these obsessions with death were making any creative activity a symptom of the terminal illness.

'Perhaps after all les tribus can act as the political force needed now – even if they are not strictly speaking a progressive minority, but in every sense peripheral. This city is wearing me away – this merry-go-round of coffee-house debate, the emblems of a revolt so furtive that it becomes self-parody – the centre laid out in series of closed compounds – slaughter houses, donkey parks, police stations, prison yards, the courtyards of mosques, everywhere precincts for waiting, coercion, suffering. 'Steady! We have not fled …' but in fact how pleasant to escape from this prison: certainly, until the prisoners are liberated we share their confinement. But even if there is simply a chance of a holiday with les tribus, how good that would be.'

Two men passed him, carrying the carcase of a fat animal: one of them waved part of its insides at him, and the other laughed. 'There, that's what it's all about. If you've any fine thoughts, friend, remember this is where they come from. My old pal Aldar here served me well, ate everything I gave him, swelled up like a tree; and then, when our relationship was at its height, as you might say, when we both happiest, he had to go and be cut up. Have a happy life, friend, and don't eat everything you're given: stay on the lean side …'

In a dusty courtyard, among dejected mules and donkeys, Osman could see three sergeants and a private performing a recruiting dance, while two sergeants and a corporal squatted watching them. A bagpiper, in white felt from head to foot, was playing for them – badly, Osman thought. Two wrestlers in black leather trousers were greasing themselves with corn oil from tins: ‘A gift from the people of the United States: not for sale.’ Two more wrestlers had started their preliminary dance, and were capering about, taking care not to look at each other.

So, thought Osman, I too am afraid of living, or of not being able to live, in a mode I myself have created. Perhaps Shala is right about les tribus, that they have been tested, they have a collective personality with which they are reasonably satisfied, and that Sadik and I have to make up in sensibility what we lack in experience …’

The corporal came up to Osman: ‘Are you afraid?’

He was burnt almost purple from the desert summer: his downswept moustaches reached to the brocade collar of the old imperial tunic which the dismounted cavalry still wore.

‘Sure, my friend. I’m afraid. So should we all be afraid.’

‘I have been on campaign among les tribus all the summer. Harassment. Relocation. I have tamed a hawk in the desert. Our artillery hits a man from ten kilometres. Are you afraid? If we kill a man of les tribus, out of kindness we kill his wife and children. I have been in the desert for three years. I am a damned man – and are you afraid?’

‘I am afraid because you still have the capacity to fear yourself.’

‘I am the tallest man in the regiment: I am seven feet tall. When I dance “scattering the sparks”, generals relax. In my village I owned a grove of apricot trees: two horses rattled their hooves against the hives. In the summer the dust rose from our threshing floor so that it looked like the stream

"Yellow". I spent the winters in a leather sack on top of the stove. I was the best singer in the village. Are you afraid?'

'Yes.'

The corporal went back to watch the dance: he looked back at Osman, and asked his question once more by raising his eyebrows, and making a half-gesture, almost like a child's, unformed.

*

'Yes, "What a marvellous old fool you are," the general told me,' said the old club servant proudly. 'That shows figures of authority here aren't made of cardboard. Why, there are some in this country afraid of their own government! Can you believe that? I've seen young officers coming to the club for fifty years, and there's never been a cross word. They tell me everything they've been doing; now it's les tribus causing trouble … always someone. But they've a sure way with them, my lads,' the old man laughed, and in this rattle of phlegm Osman smelt a sharp prickle of garlic.

'They tie the men to scout-cars and drive about the desert till they've passed over, if you get my meaning. Still, as I say, they're all human beings – as good as you, I dare say – and we've all got to live. But this insurgency thing – makes no sense: "a turquoise in the silver sand", they call this city. Why, there's everything in it a man could want: there's dark brown cheese, sheep with orange fleece, donkeys that tell your fortune by picking a card – there's even the radio for the gentlemen. You'd need to be strange to lack for anything here. Why, I sleep under the table in the officers' bar, eat in their kitchen: why should I worry? What can anyone do to me? They gave me this for carrying drinks.'

He poked out a steel claw like a crab's and with his other hand clicked it open and shut.

'Slips over the rim of a glass in a trice,' he intoned. 'No active citizen can afford to dispense with it.'

He stared at Osman with eyes like pearls, daring or exhorting him to contradict. And again Osman was frightened by the ease with which people communicated with him and by this disclosed their distance from him. His life seemed transparent, fragile, and as he walked about the city, he felt himself a translucent beetle with a blood poisonous to predators – inedible, yet monstrously vulnerable.

'Spartacus crushed?' he muttered, and laughed.

And yet, back in the observatory, when he heard Sadik discussing recruitment, and the incidence of political discussion in the cafés, it seemed that after all he had returned to a central point. To watch Shala and Curzon discussing the potential of their affection, and seeing this discussion tantalisingly, titillatingly, increasing it, appeared to him not tedious, but hopeful, serious. Shala's angry face and precise, irritated gestures could change to a smile, a tranquillity like a leaf turned over on the branch by a breeze, from copper to silver.

'Curzon will come to les tribus – but Sadik insists on staying here.'

'For whose reasons are you going?' asked Osman.

'His reasons are now the same as mine.'

'I found a loose end of the dialectic, and it led me to Shala,' said Curzon.

'I don't think that after all this need be disastrous – or no more so than anything else,' said Sadik. 'So long as we keep contact.'

And suddenly it seemed clear to Osman that at last Curzon had found a way of accepting that he loved Shala, but that this required that he cease to idealise his own existence. As far as Shala was concerned, he was not sure that to her Curzon was other than an essential peripheral phenomenon. Like light in a room, once guaranteed, it was no longer worth talking about.

*

What a splendid girl I am, thought the new student as she climbed the conical university tower. 'Never so innocent as today …' She looked out over the turquoise domes, the storks' nests, the dusty artificial trees on Martial Square. 'I have something to take from everyone …' She stroked her silky legs. The clay lid of the observatory stood out above the foxed tin roofs of the hovels, squared and quartered by tram tracks, railway lines, dry stream beds … 'How beautiful, how tranquil…'

Some children were playing on a mound of rubbish: 'Look, I've found a kitty,' shouted one, holding something aloft. 'How sweet.'

Profiles of pigs, with their single vapid grin, were stencilled on the walls. 'Beware a plague of swine,' warned the religious posters.

'Well,' said the interrogator, 'and how have you been getting on?'

The peasant courier tried to forget the book they had been reading when he last saw them – something about

> *The smoke from the stubble-fires melted into the mist: the frogs sat on the path and croaked as if it was the end of the world. And the lilac was silver in the mist and the smoke, and a lighter silver in the moonlight. And now it was cool, and we couldn't see the rakes, the hoses, the gardeners used. And the heat, and the scent of the lilacs were less – almost gone, in fact. But what am I to do? For I have not changed …*

'I've been well, you honour,' he said. 'I can see the swallows from my room.'

'We were thinking of forgetting you: I don't think you're worth a lot to us.'

'I'd accept that, your honour. But you've maybe found something to value me for.'

'Tell me how you spend your time.'

'My room is white – so white I thought there was nothing to see in it. But after a while I could see the tracks of mice, shed wingcases of beetles, brown smudges where people had rubbed a grain of rye on the walls. Soon that room was as dark and as familiar as the woodshed at home: for days indeed it seemed as if I was sitting quietly in one of my own outhouses, mending something, looking out across the valley, across the little network of streams where the wild horses come …'

He was supporting his right arm and side, since those still felt heavier and larger than the side which had not been beaten: he imagined himself a child's whittled toy, now being hardened, despite its deformity, in the fire.

'Where do you find these landscapes?'

'The paint, your honour, is uneven – not a good job, I'd say, though myself I don't find that so important. But the shadows come out brown, violet: you can see shadows through the paint, too, of soot and stone.'

'And you thought of nothing else, all this time? Not of your family? Not of your political work?'

'I have no fears for my family: my wife will have gone to her family, or married someone else. But thank you, your honour.'

'Your land, then?'

Everything I own was in that room, your honour. The lords have taken my land, your honour.'

'You know you are liable for military service? We could send you to the army.'

'As your honour pleases.'

'Have you managed to detach yourself completely from your danger?'

'Men like us don't know things the militia wants to know. I know what I know – the wild horses, the little farm, the crop of apricots. You cannot be interested in that. All that I have, I have in my room.'

'We caught you carrying a poster …'

'If your honour remembers, there were such things everywhere in the streets: I did not know what it was.'

'We shall send you to penal service in the army.'

'Thank you, your honour: I am very fortunate.'

And silently they both agreed that this was a fair judgment.

The interrogator went home to tea. 'Very quiet today,' he said. 'I don't think it'll happen after all.'

Confined for most of the working day to the lower reaches of consciousness, Sadik and Osman would often encourage the sharpening of their perception by climbing in the twilight on to one of the observatory's ledges and observing from there the movement of the city. Curzon and Shala walked through thickets of reeds, over a dense crumble of clay tiles, to the thick grey river.

'I think the authorities have already now decided to attack not us but the peasants,' said Curzon. 'I don't think for a moment they are interested in the theoretical work we do here, or even those conventional urban activities. All the signs are that an offensive has begun or is planned against les tribus. Why should they worry about numbers, or continuity? They are aware that our movement is potentially one of masses of people who simply do not figure, do not signify, under the existing system. No one even bothers to tax them or conscript them: they simply have no historical existence – their lives are pure duration. So to destroy thousands of them has no meaning. In some curious way they identify their class enemies even though I suppose the few of us are closer, more comprehensible, to their world.

'I too believe that in some sketchy way we have managed to develop the necessary confidence, the aloofness, the self-sufficiency to launch out and to stay afloat in a new tidal sea,' said Osman. 'Look at Curzon and Shala: there's a ramshackle enough relationship – but they're just able to keep it going until such time as Shala can take Curzon to les tribus. I think we're probably only able at the moment to discriminate between shades of sensibility, not between things. But I'd agree that we're as ready as we ever will be to make a decision of the order of "The revolution is now starting."'

'Certainly the rhetoric is ready,' Sadik replied, 'but we are to some extent bound by the assumptions of our urban organisation and its structure.'

'I know you want to be left in the city, Sadik. But we have urban cadres and not only is the city saturated with organisation, it's in deadlock with the police and the army. This is all you can hope to achieve: come out with us to les tribus, or you risk being caught.'

'You make us sound very much like gentlemen revolutionaries.'

Osman shrugged.

'Let's drink on it.'

They watched the pricks of diamond light in the railway sidings where welders were putting thin armour on police buses: a troop of cavalry rattled back in time for dinner. Their commander wondered whether he should extend the line of his moustaches.

If only, thought Curzon, one could acquire a memory filled with successes one had not experienced. Or, like an archaeologist, find a truly simple dialectical memory, with city piled on anti-city, pillage on preservation …

One day they heard youths shouting, 'The herds are coming.'

'We ought to contact the herdsmen,' said Sadik. 'They're influential, they circulate throughout the region, and they have connections with the settled peasants and les tribus.'

Soon they could see dusty lorries bumping in front of the herds, like scared hares.

'This is a purely social occasion,' said Osman. 'The herdsman like to meet every so often, and they have to bring along hundreds of thousands of animals.'

In the lorries were women and children: after them came herdsmen on ponies, knitting as they rode, and occasionally flinging wide their arms when they saw a friend. The animals themselves represented all stages of inbreeding and crossbreeding. They seemed to have been packed so closely together that sheep merged into goats, cattle into donkeys: there were thin cows with coats of astrakhan, sheep with twiglike horns, goats which brayed.

Some animals had heads so heavily armoured with bosses of horn that they could scarcely raise them, and wandered along like shattered warlords, staring at the ground. Others rolled their sad eyes, waving their single splintered finger of horn foolishly. They raised a mist of dust as they plodded along, too intent and too closely thronged to be interested in more than the occasional bellow or squeal. On all sides the city was besieged by multitudes of animal derivatives, looking as if a flotilla of arks had been suddenly unpacked after several millennia on the high seas. Jostling like sick rats, the herds fastened on to what vegetation they could find while their drovers came to sit over tea and grapes in the waste land by the railway sidings.

'What's the use of all these animals?' complained one of the herdsmen, a tea-caddy at his belt, dressed in thick white woollen tunic and sheepskin trousers. 'That's what I say, what's the use?'

'Why do you say that?' asked Osman.

'Degenerate lot, not a brain between the four of them. No inventiveness. No sophistication. Just sweat and chew every day of their lives – every day of my life.'

'Have you seen any military activity in the grazing areas?'

'Sure. We've all been disarmed. They've used mortars against les tribus. But I'm worried about my immortal soul, among all these sheep – not a soul among the four of them.

'Another man joined them: 'The collapse of the animal kingdom, just like grandfather said. The hierarchy, the castes, of the animals has been undermined.'

A third objected: 'In the Soviets they have good animals. It's feeding and the breeding you need.'

But the other two shook their heads. 'The heart is going out of the herds.'

The third man turned to Osman and said, 'It's the selling: there's too many nameless beasts, and the villagers won't kill them off. In any case, the herds are part of the standing debt of the peasants. The herds own the peasants, that's what it comes to.'

'What can I do to help?' asked Osman.

'If you want to help us and les tribus, it's arms we need,' said one, laughing.

'Why are you laughing?'

'Why are you asking us questions?'

'I might have arms you could use.'

They left Osman, but one said, 'It's the sign we need: as for arms, well, "look in the sand, everything is there", as you might say.'

Later, it became clear to them that the congress of herdsmen had changed its character: it had become a political gathering. 'We've been passed over again,' said Sadik, as they stood together watching the little groups of squatting men talking, whittling spinning tops, telling stories, composing crude ghazals.

'The herdsmen won't accept leaders,' remarked Shala.

Meanwhile, the herds grunted and shifted uneasily in their sickly sleep, like a vast intestine encircling the city. 'Shala, I think your intuition is gorgeous,' said Curzon.

'Won't you hold my hand?'

There were apples in light blue faience on a ground of darker blue, hinting at a translucence which lets you see their pips inset in the flesh – and the fathers and sons of those pips in ghost form around the live blue of the centre.

'Built at excessive expense and to a persistent shortfall of satisfaction by men whose perpetual serfdom could only be an inadequate reprimand for a job thoroughly botched', ran the inscription on the entrance to the mausoleum. Shala and Curzon used to meet to talk there, since the observatory was always crowded, and the more obscure corners always filled with creatures fleeing and slithering to escape the light.

The complex of mausolea sprang up in a deserted quarter outside the city, sprouting domes and broken towers as if they were vegetables running riotously to seed. But there were ripple walls to catch the sun on the waves, as it were, of an unglazed sea: in the gardens around the mausolea were shrubs whose leaves, forever in rude health, crumbled into eucalyptus and hallucination.

There were animals, and fruit trees so old and arcane that their fruits appeared without preliminary blossom, like rose-sweet jellies. The decoration on the tombs repeated these motifs: on porcelain tiles there were even a few heretical scenes of scholars selecting leaves from the shrubs,, smoking or chewing them, or designing machines – usually like copper stills – for smoking the harsh seeds. In the decoration, the animals were cool and chaste: small trees like peacocks' tails shielded smaller peacocks, calligraphy, notional flowers. With a despairing bathos, one craftsman had shown himself hiking into exile with a baby fox and some sacks of the sticky leaves, leaving behind a crumbling and ill-conceived structure.

'I suppose close contact precludes boredom,' said Curzon, 'but I'm sure you'll be thoroughly bored when the process of our tendency to detachment reasserts itself.'

'I feel that all you judgments about yourself are made for posterity, and set in terms of a classical ordering of virtues and vices. It is as if you were writing your biography, instead of living your life: at worst you are concerned with syntax rather than meaning, and at best you seem to be striving for a statement which will move and excite your audience, irrespective of what it does to you. I'm glad you're not a mirror, purely reflective and reflexive – but why aspire to be a distorting mirror?'

'I think one should pull off qualitative strokes of good living after extensive study of other people, and intensive study of one's own capacity …'

Shala said angrily, 'I've never heard anyone say "one should", "one's own" and distance themselves so much from any hope of ever themselves being that "one". It's not even intense subjectivity – it's nearer intense objectivity: as if someone supremely selfish decided to be selfish as a horse or a table, instead of as themselves. You're completely successful at effacing yourself – and yet when one searches about, there's a rich and strange personality flitting about. And absurdly enough it's gesticulating to attract attention!'

'I suppose if one is devious and all-inclusive, one must also be secretive and self-excluding. If you include all explanations, you must include the explanation that there isn't one. And other nonsense.'

'I shouldn't mind,' said Shala, 'if you admired your privacy for the sake of privacy: but you want to proselytise!'

'For the sake of sanity,' said Curzon, 'there are better things to discuss than my inner contradictions – inevitably though these will lead to my decline and fall. I have a cuddly side as well as the cerebral.'

'I suppose it is flattering, to know you're having all conceivable relationships with me, in addition to the one I think we're having. But this way it's hard to surprise you – and I'm rather attached to my own single affection for you. In any case, I'm not sure that this crushing and crashing self-knowledge is good for you. In increases your powers of perceptions to such an extent that the power to discriminate disappears altogether.'

'By all means – so after all, it's just cheap sensation I'm after. A pity my historical context won't allow me to enjoy anything but middling to expansive sensation.'

'I feel it's just ingrowing: you're only concerned with symptoms, ever more vestigial ones. I think you'd hate a cure.'

'But isn't this making the symptoms more interesting? Didn't I catch you with symptoms? A healthy mind in a sick body? A healthy mind in a healthy mind? Don't forget – "Who/whom?" If this is self-absorption, then it's got you interested – so, many thanks to my symptoms – and since these are possible choices, or motives attributed to actual choices, I can always stop thinking about them, and they'll go away, as it were. Which would you prefer me as – a deluder, or self-deluded? You get both for the price of one.'

'Fair enough – but where do I disappear in this acrobats' nightmare? You're out on stage, grunting and puffing as more and more of your athletic multiple attributes leap into each others' shoulders – or shoulder, perhaps – but what is my role? Do I just steady the great schizoid pyramid, in case it falls on me? Or am I your claque? I don't like being a figment of one of the tributaries of your consciousness.'

'Yes, that does seem the weakness of what I really intended to be a conceit – a rationalisation of diffidence and a strict upbringing, perhaps? But this is all rather silly because I really do love you.'

'Do you?'

They had seen that morning their first guerrilla casualty: a man carried in from the desert, lying on a stretcher, knees drawn up, as if prepared for some prehistoric burial. He had breathed in sharply at the moment of death, and his expression was neither of pain nor surprise: it seemed indeed as if he had determined to leave no message on his face to be mocked or remembered: it said merely 'in progress'. His body was put on show in the main square, surrounded by police camions.

Osman whispered to Shala, 'He was lucky, that was a quiet and unimportant way to die – and an important use to have made of him now. It's as if a new ore had been discovered in the desert and put on show with a notice saying, "We think this is gold. Citizens are requested not to look for any more."'

Shala dropped on the body a few blue and yellow petals. By the end of the day the corpse was buried under flowers. She said, 'I fear torture, and I fear mutilation after death, because I am terrified of hatred. To die like this man, that's nothing. But then my consciousness has taken no forms which could lead it to want to continue through oblivion – especially if I could feel I'd had some political effect. I feel my own four walls, or I'm nothing: my consciousness is only of the moment, my sensations, even the sensation of past sensations, are not transmittable – not even in the form of ghosts. But you must feel that your poetry has extended your consciousness?'

'I don't know what you mean – but I understand what you're asking. Yes, in a sense to write is a constant and absorbing pleasure, and the results are like mental photographs, pleasant to take out and lie about. But I am more realistic and exact about oblivion than you. What I've written has in some sense satisfied me – and perhaps you envy me this: what I've yet to compose presses on me, and this is always exciting and challenging. It's like being an isolate bee in a big but rather sparsely furnished hive, with his own secret store of ready-made honey. It is the price one pays, and also the reward, for isolation.'

'It seems to me that Curzon stands in the way of happiness – but perhaps after all this is too simplistic. To believe that fulfilment is only dependent on contingent things is to admit not to complete self-adjustment, but complete powerlessness over the important features of one's environment.'

Osman laughed. 'I wonder what the guerrilla would say. For my part I understood that I should probably die in the same way. My only problem was to make sure I had a sufficient impetus not to mind about it. Sadik organises, Curzon torments himself with love and desire, and the history of his class and childhood, I write marginally better ghazals than before. I don't claim anything for my methods – I've not been transformed: I was pretty well-rounded before I came here with you all. All that has happened is that in order to keep the fullness full, as it were, sudden death has become a necessary condition of my continued existence. I don't intend that as a paradox, or a reasoned statement: it's just accurate, and doesn't bother me.

'You, Shala, are in a much worse position. You can only deal in cataclysms – you need at least one a year. And yet although you accept that cataclysms create deserts and wreck libraries, you can't see that the bones in the sand were once inside tormented bodies. You expect things to have a harsh and rigorous existence, and people to go from strength to strength.'

'Do you think I idealise les tribus, then?'

'No! What you tell us about them is marvellous. I'm longing to go out there. If the description works for you, I'm sure with a little concentration it will work for the rest of us.

Curzon will share your concepts because he wishes to enter into your imagination – I don't think he admires your intellect. Sadik will enjoy political work there because it's a step nearer to the confrontation he is seeking. You'll enjoy it because we each in our own devious ways will agree that we should have gone earlier and trusted you …'

'Well, there's my comeuppance!'

'I don't mean it to be. In any case, these habits of thought and experience divide us superficially: we all try to come closer to each other. But the political work we are doing is the central and collective activity: the rest is the essential "everything else".'

That evening men came with torches and set them up in memory of the unknown guerrilla: the gleam of the flares on the petals turned the whole bier to flame.

'If a few of us have the chance to write our own scripts, I don't think we should mind also being cast in them – even if we can't play the roles we are assigned, and resent always being killed off in the first scene,' said Sadik.

He and Shala were watching a military parade – a kind of parody of 'Lenin on the platform'. A band was playing the *marche militaire* as it is played in hell: the bandsmen had unrolled their instruments, and the creased yellow tubes waved and honked like the trunks of jaundiced elephants. Slithering and sliding with diabolic virtuosity the players produced a jagged dance of almost sulphurous savagery. A tall, armless general stood saluting with his strong claw.

'This is a bit too much,' whispered Shala. 'No one would have dared to write a script like this.'

Soldiers in motley ran past the saluting base: some charged down the streets with fixed bayonets, while others – from a desert assault regiment – crawled past interminably and cautiously.

'What an empty conceit,' said a man in front of them in the crowd. 'When I was with the white patriots in 1920, we crawled in the desert and it was like inching over a charcoal grill. I'd like to have seen the emperor trying that – he'd have bubbled like a toad on the hearth!'

'Like a toad on the hearth' – Sadik heard the crowd seize the words and toss them to and fro, with an uneasy mixture of amusement and menace.

'Where's the lorries then?' cried a woman. 'Who's had the lorries? And who's had my Istvan's dinner these thirty years? What do they do with all the lorries, and all the men they take out into the desert? And the food we grow, and the kittens we don't drown. Who's been eating my Istvan's dinner, then?'

The general, with one arm still firmly at the salute, waved at the woman furiously with the other.

'It was you, it was you, then,' the crowd shouted back delightedly.

'They don't seem overawed,' said Shala. 'Perhaps in a way they ought to be.'

Together they walked away from the scornful and complacent crowd, happy in its certainty that the army would flow by safely, never climbing its banks, never wetting a foot or flooding a bolthole. Shala sat on the clay saucer rim of an ur-tomb – filled with the unlocked bones of animals: 'We are living in a world of untamed and unclassified concepts. Some mornings it seems an act of bravery to walk about in such an unordered world, where prediction is at the level of the most naked coercion or sorcery.'

'Surely,' said Sadik, 'you have to decide whether you want scientific communism or critical communism – to escape from the tyranny of things or the tyranny of concepts. That's my reading of things, anyway. I can never decide what my tactical work is tending towards: I think probably its value lies in a layer of conventions, signs, symbols, scraps of dialogue, so dense and so mixed that it's like a sort of living cosmic brawn. But tell me, Shala, how much longer are we to have your poignant, yearning, churning affair with Curzon? You know how much I like you – how much I like you both. We seem already to have so much death around, even to think of happiness is brave.

'I promise you I don't criticise you, or say you're self-indulgent. But where does this figure? I mean, where does your love, if you are calling it love, help you or anyone else? And please don't tell me that love is a universally negotiable and honoured currency – because it isn't, here, for instance. I'm not asking because I want to stop you being in love, or because it may be dangerous or because I've a desire for whatever reason to see you finish with it. I'm just interested: why now? How important is it? What do you expect from your feelings? What can you give each other in the next few weeks apart from the impression that where your life stops, the life of someone else, somebody you love, begins. That's fair enough, as a physical description, and I can see in a sentimental way that you'll have comfort, something to think about and so on. But what's more?'

'I think that's too schematic, Sadik. You're a debunking romantic, and despite all this interest in stable and magnificent relationships, I'm not sure why you should start believing that long means deep.'

'I think you're getting away by being more rigorously schematic. I suppose basically you attract me strongly and I enjoy any kind of chit-chat with you – but I believe I can't concentrate on my private feelings until things are more secure.'

'I'm glad you want me to wait, Sadik. And I'm glad that I'm not just flattered – if indeed I'm flattered at all – by what you've said.'

Women from les tribus were waiting for the buses to take them within range of their settlements. They looked like rich fruit, striped, feather-barred, waving huge stylised switches of horses' tails to chase away the flies. 'You're surely not going to take that foal on the bus?' one asked. 'The city seems so stark and austere: I think my little boy would like a horse of his own.'

'The menace here is so strong, I think we should all get horses. Over at Kharazbad they brought up mortars and said we should move. They said they were making a survey – but they've set up a park for lorries.'

In the city the flames burning over the mass graves had gone out: every day, petty official embezzlers made their coups and set off for the coast – at best for a lifetime of discomfort in the French provinces, at worst for a few furtive months of illusion before the next currency reform. Artistic demonstrations now easily outnumbered political ones: students, folk singers, musicians and actors from every folk, national, popular, class and regional culture rediscovered the principles of their art, and contested their criteria with dragon dances.

Some aesthetes affected the costumes of the Thermidorians, and hit passers-by with small cudgels. There were even attempts to fuse all these elements into one – but the mixture was so rich, so exotic, so savage, whimsical, fluid, chemical, so acid-sugary, that at once its converse was created – a synthetic compound of a crackling originality and spontaneity. Partisans of each carried their battles to the very walls of the temporary barracks, the auxiliary police stations, the field hospitals.

A bus called 'Old Shiraz' drew up: 'Why call it that? grumbled the woman with the strawberry-coloured foal.

'I think this is all a matter of the expectation of the length of one's creative life,' said Osman. 'In a way, while this is very much as if cultural seed pods, built to lie dormant for centuries, had suddenly burst, I think most of my colleagues are fully aware what kind of permanent change they can expect and can resist. They are for the most part aware of where experiment ends and ingestion begins. But I'm not sure myself what all this is a by-product of.'

'Need one suggest,' asked Curzon, 'that this is the way the attack on les tribus makes itself felt on the skin of our culture? It's a sort of prickly heat, an itch which needs soothing, but gets nothing but more heat, more scratching …'

'You're very organic today.'

'Only inside my head. Don't accuse me of such heresy that I should believe that some kind of mind sends messages to my brain – and that my brain then thinks about them before storing them in my mind again.'

'But Curzon, isn't this true? The most physical thing about you is your imagination. The rest is ephemeral. We won't ever need to bury you, you'll just fade like memory. When we think of you – there you'll be again until we forget you again.'

'You sound like Shala.'

'No, not really. I admire you for this detachment: I think it right that you should have become detached from Elizabeth, from the bourgeoisie and its modes, and all that. I'm glad you put your intellect at the service of les tribus, of our working-class. I can see that you know how valuable this was. If you do nothing better than this, it will still mean that you understand emancipation, even if you cannot free your body from the chains which have been put on it, and even if you cannot free your body from the chains which have been put on it, and even if your mind in fact puts further constraints on your body. I don't even want to get you thinking about your mental liberation, because this will stop you acting – you really will become pure thought.'

'In the morning when I write up the campaign diary, I have each day to invent a new cypher based on the previous day's entry, which in turn refers back to the first one of all – arbitrary and unintelligible to anyone but me. It's rather like having a collection of eighteenth-century gramophone records: common sense says you can't have – but once transcend the initial impossibility and you have something quite unremarkable, predictable and banal. I think all of us who straddle two historical or social forms look pretty ridiculous afterward – and that in itself is as it should be. The thing to do is to get the transition over as quickly as possibly – there's nothing worse than hanging fire for a couple of centuries.'

They went back to the observatory: 'One of the flying foxes frightened Shala yesterday.'

'What do you expect, Osman?' asked Curzon.

'I hope for a succession, a gathering, of people like Shala. If this makes me more selfish than you, then it makes me kinder. Again, if my imagination has not the same heights as yours, then at least I don't doubt my capacity to do the best I can – and I think you have trouble in believing this about yourself.'

'Let's have some drink,' said Curzon.

They sat in the litter of oiled paper which the arms were wrapped in, the bones of creatures from the largest to the infinitely receding, and the millennial deposit of glazed pottery tiles.

'There's a kind of swamp near the pipeline at the coast: I often would go there all day to drink wine. They'd a yellow wine that was more green, and red wines that were closer to blue, and to black. In the evening, either the water went down, or plants grew upwards to enjoy the coolness. For throughout the day, there was nothing on the surface but the snouts of buffalo. But when the sun began to sink, up would come the roses, the thistles, from the lake bed, throwing out from their tightly clenched buds scarlet and blue flowers.

'By this time my consciousness was so expanded it had begun to lose its density in patches. "My rose, my rose but your thorns are bitter." I used to sit there by the stinking mud, humming that song, and feeling as happy as if I'd thought of it all myself. And indeed, it still seems to me now as if I was always the same when I went there, the wine never bit me, the flowers opened up in the same way, at the same time: and always there was the same boredom, followed by the same engrossing detachment and companionship – and then the return to happiness as a secret vice.

'In the end I felt it all so sentimental I had to stay home. I couldn't tell anyone why I slipped away to run through my emotional resources in the course of a day – they would either have laughed, or wanted to come too. So I sat there drinking, listening to the local musicians, talking to the boatmen in their astrakhan caps, while they curled their moustaches.'

'I think,' said Curzon, 'I should have had both reactions – that this was unbearably sentimental, and that I wanted to come too. But that says less for me than for you.'

They were discussing the last pages of the Russian girl's diary – the day the peasants broke down the walls of the garden, and set fire to the outhouses. The fire spread –

> *even the lilac trees were burning with a hungry flame that would never be put out, a flame running over the almond trees, overleaping the brooks filled still with pebbles like pigeons' eggs – burning everything on its way to the village. And beyond the village there were other fires, and in the sky too, alleys of fire: and hot and cold, it was all fire, and all darkness, with the black smoke hiding the flames, and the flames lighting up – darkness …*

'It's very strange,' said Shala, 'the photographs of the peasants in those months seem to show them as stern, or shy, or happy. Poor girl – the only way she could come to terms with them and herself was by passionately desiring her own destruction. In order to secure the liberation she needed, the had to play her tiny role in supporting a system which had to be smashed, and her with it – she had to be victim in the very moment she appeared as tyrant. I'm beginning to understand what the peasants here mean when they say they're not interested in politics. They mean that for them to avoid politics is to avoid massacre: for us, politics is the only way of trying to avoid massacre.'

Curzon thought of Elizabeth's last letter:

> *I've been thinking as much about what we ought to do – both of us, I mean, darling. Since I've been back, I feel you'll never be decisive enough to commit yourself to anything you don't fully agree with. I think in our lives, that that 'something' is the way I understand you – I think you need me to understand you, and that this is something for you to cling to. Indeed, it's the only thing you'll ever have to cling to.*

This terrible threat squeaked away at Curzon, a minute transmitting device whispering out a permanent signal of recall, capitulation – the unattended press turning out countless copies of the order to surrender while the generals themselves were making for the woods like foxes.

'I should like to be more austere,' said Curzon.

'That is not possible. Your only concern seems to be with your own refinement – and I think you're wrong to think that grossness is to be avoided at all costs. You're a bit like a slug that won't leave a trail: if you wish to slither about, as a decent and normal slug you have no choice but to leave a trail.'

'Thank you: that puts it perfectly.'

'But,' said Shala, 'you think because a thing can be put into words, that's the end. To you it is only consciousness which signified, and you don't just believe this, you set it out.'

A red bird, with a rattle in its throat like a clock spring, whirred twice, and waited for beetles to come running.

All day now there seemed to be cold clouds fleeting over the city: 'We must collect some donkeys if we are going to les tribus,' said Curzon. Men from ethnic minorities so tiny that they themselves had no name for them, came to the slums by the city walls to escape the winter. They brought with them a savage culture which frightened the townsmen: they made music from the gourds and bones they found in the refuse tips of the desert, singing with bitterness and self-mockery in fierce nasal voices.

*

They saw a great deal of one man dressed in a smock marked 'All-Union Record Factory' who used to declaim in some disused language – perhaps so arcane that he had forgotten the original and re-invented a tongue known only to himself. It was only after several days that they realised that the declamation consisted of questions, not statements: this relentless, unanswerable inquiry went on into the night, always ending with a hopeless, helpless, 'Ayay' after midnight, and the one Persian obscenity he had learned.

As the memory of the summer host faded, so that light became still sharper: the crowd of les tribus at the bus terminus now wore quilted jackets, from which peeped the young lynxes – too young to be left at home. But no one was interested in the training of the animals and the description of their racing. In the tea-houses the pottery benches filled with charcoal were brought out. In the streets a man went round shooting the dogs which might become wild when food ran short. The schools are closed – for want of fuel, it was said. The gutters were full of leaflets – 'How many years, comrades?', 'The refined sensibility of the padishah', 'The delights of police persecution'.

'They always seem to have one last day of racking heat here before the winter,' said Osman. 'It kills off the plants quicker than a frost.' And indeed, the sun on one day exhausted the thick green flowering shrubs which had successfully gone over to a winter economy: the trees with juicy leaves as broad as hands were blasted and withered. Within a few hours, the parks were full of a decaying pulp of vegetation. By midday miasma had risen halfway up the city walls. There was a smell of rotting gourds and marrows, the warm putrefaction of mutton and jam, and the thin carrion waft from outside the walls of melon skins, eggshells and dust.

In the desert the sun knocked over the carefully hoarded beasts of les tribus: the animal surplus was destroyed in a few hours, leaving the scorched corpses of the late lambs and retarded foals on which the children had lavished so many vain hopes.

'This is a day of ultimate frustration,' said Shala. 'We always feel that during the summer we have come to terms with the environment. The peasants think that despite increases in debts and rent, they've managed to hide enough away to live comfortable through the winter. And then in a few hours, despite every precaution, we find that, after all, the rents and the debts were precisely calculated. For this day of heat turns the hidden wine sour, blights the fruit and melts the cheese, dries up the honey in the hives. So everyone is forced to live badly during the winter, and to start the same old fraudulent race again in the spring.'

'Refrigeration is contrary to God's wishes,' the patriarch told his tape recorder: 'Clearly this day of punishment is referred to in every major religion. Better the heat than another form of disaster. For God in his infinite wisdom is infinitely ingenious when it comes to conceiving of new blights and illnesses. So don't get above yourselves, you heathen,' he added. 'Poor suffering humanity,' he whispered. 'Where would I be without your poverty, your suffering, your humanity?'

With complexity and deviousness, and for the sake of a succession of devious and interlaced transactions, physical and meditative declines, two old men beat out with bells, clappers, and two small drums that looked like brown cheeses, a rhythm of meandering cross reference and nullity.

'I think we're getting caught up too much in the specific and the accidental,' said Curzon. 'We should find our base with les tribus. And yet I'm afraid of committing myself – of sacrificing the comfortable, illusory freedom of indecision for the hardness and austerity of the liberation from which only extinction, not hesitation, can come as fulfilment.'

'You don't seem to anticipate many incidental rewards,' said Shala. 'Liberation means raising desire to a higher level, and even if you fulfil this desire, in that very moment you extinguish your enjoyment of liberation …No one can say you flatter your friends, or yourself!'

'There's a tenderness in sadness discussed in pleasant company. In any case it would probably be more realistic to see ourselves shattered by the militia rather than by a passion.'

'As if all the telephone lines in the world had ended, and the air was filled with unchannelled, undirected manages: 'I do not want you.' 'I do not know you.' And yet even this is to dignify – if only with bathos – what is probably a mechanical breakdown – whose weakest link in the causal chain was someone wholly admirable or likeable, who forgot to replace a switch or a fuse because he was drunk, or thinking of something else. And, after all, our critique of our would-be masters is only necessary and possible so long as they master us – we must be careful lest in sharpening our critique we forget the task of refining our own sensibility …'

They passed through the austere quarter of the city: a fierce hinterland where two faiths met, the children screamed hymns at their creed enemies, and the unemployed stood helplessly outside the 'Boyne Bridge Inn'.

Finally, Osman told Curzon: 'We feel you need to keep on making upward spirals in your consciousness and in your practice. You think you have to jump once – you don't.

Especially you – you must keep transcending your past not only intellectually, but in action and in commitment.'

'Does Sadik accept this?' asked Curzon. 'I should have thought this thinking would disrupt all his organisation.'

'Yes, in a way Sadik has to work as a vulgar materialist. We all do sometimes, but he shares our methodology, while you soon increasingly to share only an abstract admiration for it, and for yourself. You want to lead for a little while, and be proud of yourself. Then everyone will catch you up, and you'll have a ready-made status, and can let everyone revere you. But this is vulgar – too vulgar for Shala, I promise you.'

'Isn't Shala a complication?'

'In the sense that she's your complication. If Shala increases your effectiveness – then I'm delighted. And if she increases your happiness – then I'm no more and no less happy. But if you stop jumping, you're finished, you're a dead twig.'

A little later, Osman said, 'I'm sorry for the dead twigs – but I can do nothing with them or they for me, or for anyone.'

He returned to the subject later in the day. 'You above all cannot afford to drop behind. If it is true that you live most fully in cerebration, then there will be no comfort and no satisfaction in deciding to freeze your commitment at some point. You must reject everything you do, everything you write, the moment you seem to be imprisoned within it. Perhaps with les tribus you will find the dialectic in action and be swept up on its broad back,' and he laughed.

I only hope, thought Curzon, that it is Osman and Shala who survive, and not me.

Gingerbread tigers were paraded through the streets, and then distributed to the poor. Sadik had tried to persuade everyone not to accept. 'We have the majority – but we're not crystallising it,' he said. 'They all accept my case – but they still eat the gingerbread. If only there had been no tigers this year…'

A young man came up to them, his face varnished with gingerbread. 'See, this was my girl.' He produced a photograph of a girl on a horse – the face and uplifted arm out of focus, two white bean-shaped blobs. Still, for a moment she had left this shadow for him, a gesture anonymous and poignant, to be carefully filed alongside the banknotes and return tickets.

'We were in the Soviet Union,' he added wistfully. 'The barley smelt of carnations, and we had all the jam we could eat.'

'Don't you feel,' asked Sadik, 'that you're a bit oppressed here? It can't be much of a life to get a gingerbread dole, and be sent off into the desert against les tribus. Don't you feel like asserting yourself – you and your comrades?'

'We don't mind. It all seems reasonable enough.'

Osman said later, 'The word for reason and for "here" are the same.'

'With a theory of consciousness,' said Curzon, 'the trouble seems to be that we must be authoritarian – because we have more developed consciousness – until we control education.'

'I don't think we could be described as authoritarian now,' said Osman. 'And you're wrong about education. There is a problem about infrangible modes of course …' They stopped for a while outside a taxi-dance: a group of local musicians – bagpipers, drummers – alternated with a band more westernised, its cymbals tisking, its clarinet bubbling like a bird in Macedonia.

'How sad they all look,' said Shala. 'Only the musicians can successfully blend their traditions. They do so for practical reasons, and because they are bored with the old. But the dancers – are the men to dance with the women? Should there be women with the men at all? Everyone is stuck between the orchestras like a weak butterfly still imprisoned in its chrysalis. Will we be in permanent transition, senile infants torn between their Proust and their first day at school?'

The peasants and townsmen on the dance-floor shyly shuffled to each other's dances. Men from les tribus took their boxwood tea-caddies to the bar and tried to buy hot water. Six peasants, hugely drunk, sat on the floor and howled like dogs. A sergeant in the militia danced a girl's dance to the applause of his charges.

'Hashish is the opium of the people,' shouted a man with goitre.

It is a pity, thought Osman, that when you are yourself the new society in the shell of the old, you can't even get drunk in the good comfortable ways of old.'

'Five kings in one,' said the man with the dice.

'This hall is called "Tuz" – "ace",'

'I remember,' said Osman, when they had bought some Armenian brandy, 'some years ago I used to cross the plain of tufa outside the port. You could see the shapes of Greek armour in the stone – these were already salt springs around the port. You could see the orange lizards with red berries in their mouths, trying to remember where were the best places to lurk. Then you came to the melon fields, then to the sandstone pillars – like toadstools. They called the place, "No-one at all" or "Abdi-Daroun's fountain" – but there's no fountain and no water,' he added.

'So how did they live?'

'They made arak from the berries. I went there a lot. They lived in a tarred barracks, and they invented lies and legends. They were rebuilding a Russian lorry they had discovered, and planned to drive east.'

'This sounds like an inconclusive story,' said Curzon.

'Well, yes, up to a point. But for years I would walk for two hours or more to clamber through the thistles and the tufa, the tumbledown terraces, to deliver some of the lies I'd thought of at the quayside. We used to sit in the hut, listening to tar blisters bursting in the midday sun, twirling with arak like the thistle-bushes from the plain. There was a man there – the first communist I ever met: we called him 'Party'. He was a better poet than I. But despite all the arak, the singing, the lies, the taxi-dance girls, the band of tufa, copper to the pink sky – all they wanted was to repair their truck.'

They drank fast and easily.

'Is it a disadvantage not to have mined for zinc or managed a lynx,' asked Curzon. 'Never to have jumped outside all the comforts which circumscribed and defined me?'

'Please, no bathos,' said Shala. 'You're catching up nicely. We've got a printing press to publish your most fleeting thoughts. When we get our arms to les tribus you will be able to help them prevent a massacre. You seem to have had a most useful preparation: after all, there aren't many others here with your background. The people you envy have not rushed to the vanguard.'

A man from les tribus plucked Sadik's sleeve. 'The old ones cannot carry on in the same way,' he whispered. 'The khakhan's guard dogs have been set on us: they are killing us, between them and us there is no distance, not the breadth of a hand. They have French self-propelling guns …'

'Surely you can see what people here feel,' said Shala when he had gone. 'They know there can never be a recovery now. If les tribus are destroyed, do you imagine the ministers could look without alarm at the mass of the population which would long ago have risen against the army and the militia if only it had the organisation, and some chance of success? We can take our arms to the desert, leave the cadres in the city – and then see what happens. Or lose everything – and almost certainly ourselves be captured …'

'We'll have to discuss it in the morning,' said Osman. 'Curse this brandy. But now we've started, we should go the whole way,' pouring honey down his throat. '*Maintenant c'est l'heure du départ …*'

Curzon had no doubt that they would go to les tribus: 'new world!' – the chance to live in the physical world, to leave the philistinism of the seminar, the taxi-dance, the observatory. Already the tide of brandy was sweeping him over blunt rocks to the open sea. He shouted to Shala, 'I am returning to the interior the hard way.'

'Five kings the hard way' – did someone say that? Absurd. And Shala was smiling at him, and the harder he embraced her the nearer she came, the warmer came her smile. He could feel the brandy making him cry, and thought, 'No bathos,' but with relief – the relaxation of decades of constraint, of feeling one thing and acting another. 'We are going to Cythera,' he told Shala as they danced laughing.

'I would not go without you. You will come if I go,' said Shala at one point, but Curzon could not remember if this was an answer to any question of his. He felt that all the people in the room cheered when he spoke, that confidence in their immediate victory was fanning back like a wake to the onlookers as he himself was drawn out to sea ever faster by the American brandy.

Osman was singing. 'Osman is singing,' he told Shala.

Speaking very slowly and clearly she said, 'You are free. We are both free,' but again he could not remember if this was a reply or part of a longer statement.

'I'll see you again, my friend,' the sergeant in the militia said. 'The nonsense out there can't last for ever.'

'What exactly do you mean?' asked Curzon.

'Some of the guard dogs are restless.' And he winked.

Later, Curzon told Shala, 'We are going to les tribus. Honey-gold, Armenian-gold girl: to les tribus – there and back again, free …'

'And not to Cythera after all?' asked Shala laughing.

'You're laughing. And yes, why not to Cythera too? Is that still Osman singing?'

'No, that's a Turkoman,' said Osman. 'This brandy is sliding down very nicely.'

'What happens when we get to the other side?' Curzon asked, referring to his trip over the sea.

'We turn round and come back.'

'But we'll still be free.'

'If that's all you want,' said Curzon, suddenly gloomy. Then, brightening, 'I think I'll go as resident, not pilgrim: no visa required.'

'This was the best evening of the whole revolution,' said Shala later. 'When the history comes out, do you think there'll be a reference? Should we make some record of it now?'

'We are our own record. And I certainly can't tell you now enough of the things I feel to make them memorable. I'll remember it all tomorrow, and start from there.'

'Perhaps I know already.'

'Well, if you use these standards, we all know what I feel and am going to say. But as you well know, what matters is not finding new things to say – but who says the old things to whom. So you'll have to suffer the boredom – it's all a part of the process …'

They galloped back to the observatory: the moonlight was so fierce they no longer needed to feel drunk. They could still hear the singing from the dance –'A nail from the shoe of the horse of the Emperor Franz'.

That's not even the right country, thought Curzon as he slowed down and began to sink into the warm sticky sea.

The first snow obliterated the colours of the city. It now looked like a badly peeled fresco. From the observatory you could see the last birds scuttling away down the sky, and some crippled soldiers toasting crusts over the eternal flames in the war memorials. A few processions, mostly of literary societies, still wound their way from the city suburbs to the offices of the censorship, but it was too cold to demonstrate, and some poets even brought copies of their clandestine work to be burnt on the squares to provide warmth.

When the townsmen put on their fur coats and hats, the summer truce with the animals seemed to have been broken – the dogs turned savage, and it was rumoured that a wolf had been shot under the city walls. The men and women of les tribus no longer came to the markets, and the compounds where they used to leave their mules now contained munitions, military supplies of all kinds. At night you could hear strings of lorries leaving for the desert, and see on the pavements faded flowers tossed out by conscripts: 'I was not consulted', 'Where?', 'I long for some apricots', said the notes crumpled round the stems.

'We seem thorough amateurs: everything we've done has been undertaken without adequate discussion and analysis…' said Curzon, as he and Sadik searched the pitiful messages the couriers had gathered.

'This is absolutely true, but fortunately no one else had been in competition with us. We've done about all we can: when there's a revolutionary situation the deficiencies in organisation will be made clear, and at the same time repaired, by hundred – and thousandfold – increases in our numbers. We could only create our cadres, no more.'

'We must at least have done enough to stop them arresting us,' said Curzon. 'They must be more afraid of a premature insurrection than of letting us swan about the city. Perhaps it's as well as we are leaving while we can.'

'Yes, we shall be moving from the sphere of one ministry to the next when we leave the city: we shall have some weeks' grace while they transfer our files.'

In the city an old mechanic wrote to his son: 'We have been witnessing some extraordinary things. The soldiers have come – but they are going to the desert. I have all the welding I can do. A man said to me, "The better you weld, the quicker they'll be back. Give them something to think about in the desert." Now, I thought, I am witnessing something difficult. Whose turn will it be next? – it might be mine. But will it be my turn earlier or later? So at first I thought: it's not for me to decide. But after a while I thought: Here's a way to get back what they've been taking off me for years. Why should les tribus suffer because I'm a good welder?

'So I did the worst work I've ever done. There's an odd feeling here – that people are taking stock of all they've ever done. What was it all worth? What benefit did we get for all our devotion? Were we really devoted to ourselves and our families – or to the landlords and the bosses? All the time we were thinking how clever and selfish we were – were we really lining someone else's pocket? Probably where you are they'll tell you different – is it true they eat lynx where you are? – but I can tell you, none of us that's here can go on as before. It's funny to think of all those welds cracking in the desert: I suppose if you'd been conscripted I'd have thought twice. My back's as crook as a plum tree.'

But his son had long ago been tried and sentenced.

A unit of militia sat in the desert dark and watched the sky on all sides fill with flaming kites. One, splayed out like a hand, began to break up, and soon the soldiers were surrounded by flames like marsh gas. A few thistle-bushes ignited and hopped away over the silver hills. The lieutenant wrote: 'Are we in the middle of them, or do they surround us? These kites are very beautiful, but the makers would do better to run away. My dearest, les tribus are so ugly – it is a positive duty to harry them! There are piles of rubble out here – I should think that when we've saved the democracy we should come back and see if it's at all valuable.

'One of the corporals broke a leg today, and I hurt my hand. How good it would be to play tennis again – I'm sure my game will be atrocious when I come back. The sergeant is an honest fellow, but so slow and plodding –and, my dear, you'd laugh – but here we are out after a lot of peasants, just like grandfather's day – and all my little company are peasants too, or workmen of the lowest sort. I remember grandfather telling me that in his day they couldn't use the peasants against the peasants, so we have something to be thankful for now.'

And the sergeant looked up at the sky and tried to work out where les tribus had come from – and whether the paintings in the mausoleum he had discovered that day were from the same school as the ones in his village.

'Obviously the decoration comes from the Mir-Arab building – but my neighbour has always said nothing as late as that really signifies …' He thought of the red, black, green bees searching his tiny pasture, the two white horses secure behind a fence of living, plaited saplings. He remembered the book he had found – letter by letter, he teased out: 'The exploits of Abdulaziz Khan, and his search for …' He was shocked by the poverty of les tribus: 'There's nothing more they can do; there's nothing here except the shells of cities men have left …' 'We should be good to the poor – but we are killing them. Besides, the officers despise us: grandfather was beaten by their guard dogs …'

Something very complicated was happening all round them. One day it would be possible to shoot the lieutenant: it wasn't possible in the barracks, but out here sergeants were more important than officers. The men would follow a sergeant because his orders came from good sense. A lot of bad things would be changed simply by killing the officers. Then they could do anything – go home, go to les tribus, use the guns against anyone who came. They could not go on in the old way – and things could not be worse. The officers did things the gentry never should: they did not kill men as equals, for money or to avenge: they did not steal, they destroyed, they did not kill, they mutilated. It was hard not to mutilate with these guns – but many of the soldiers liked the madness.

'We must be against the officers …' he mumbled.

No one heard. We must be against the officers, he thought, because they are changing us – they are changing us to be their guard dogs; soon we shall all be guard dogs. When les tribus are destroyed, we shall all be guard dogs. When I came here, I had no quarrel, no quarrel with les tribus. But the longer they resist, the more I have a quarrel. We cannot continue in the old way…'

All over the desert the soldiers looked at the kites and thought: 'the old ways are gone', and some wished they could go and exchange songs and ghazals with les tribus. Some cursed les tribus for land thieves, and cursed the thieves who, in their absence, were making off with their livestock. Others pressed their wirelesses hard to their ears, listening to the last filaments of metropolitan music, and the national anthem. Then they slept.

‘Such a pity. What starts off as a police action, degenerating into all-out military operations. If only they’d not been greedy. Be content with what you’ve got, sergeant,’ said the officer of police. ‘Though I expect you think me a vulgar materialist on the basis of that remark?’ And he laughed.

‘Well, sir, yes and no, sir.’ The sergeant, whittled and charred by razormen and arsonists over the years, carefully aimed a paperclip through the window, down fifty feet on to the helmet of the soldier on guard. ‘It’s just more work as I see it: there’s the informers, the doctor’s fees for the informers, the fees for the doctoring and the burying of the prisoners, the percentage from the new brothels – paperwork, all paperwork.’

‘Poor old sergeant,’ giggled the officer, ‘seen it all before, have you? Never mind, you know then, that it all ends the same old way.’

Not always, you primping old shark, thought the sergeant. One day we’ll hoist you up in the sky and juggle you till your false fangs dash on the ground – no more mock piety, no more mock guts. I’d make les tribus hop. One day we’ll put the peasants in the villages and the townsmen in the towns: we’ll put the books in the library, and the tourists in the tourist hotel. And anything that moves, we’ll interrogate.

‘Listen to this, sergeant. “Ladies and gentlemen of the press – how kind of you to come all this way to our beautiful city. The people have every confidence in the army and the police. The army and the police have every confidence in the people.

No problem. You may be misled – you may think we are attacking les tribus. This is absurd: Article 12 of the Constitution guarantees access to the land: estates over ten thousand hectares and rents above forty per cent are illegal.

'"If you find a thief in your back garden, ladies and gentlemen, you invoke the law. We are enforcing that law. Les tribus are led by foreigners, supplied from abroad. They do not deserve even your pity – indeed, you may be sure that we are more merciful than you ... There are cakes, souvenirs, and trips to the battle-zone to be had ... Let us hope that democracy may one day flourish in the desert – if I may be poetical – as it does in this police barracks ..." How's that, sergeant?'

'Marvellous, sir,' he dropped a second paperclip. When I've dropped seventy thousand, he thought, we'll get things moving. Aloud, 'What about these rumours of Englishmen, arms and the like?'

'It's a good rumour to keep simmering away. Load of nonsense. How boring it all is – a little insect man with ideas boiling away like formic acid: if only they knew how silly it looks, how unavailing. Let's talk about structurally differentiated elites, systems, anti-systems – but as for finding new things to say about freedom, rents, landlords – it's the twittering of grasshoppers, butterflies, the in-and-out flickering of lizards. How very, very, boring!' And he and the sergeant smiled at each other.

*

Our movement is capillary: it is spreading through the trades and industries like oil on water. It binds together: it is its nature to spread. Do you have your freedom, your justice, under the present system? If so, use it to protect les tribus. If not – you will ask whether a new order would be better. Well, a new order is coming: it is for you to be active in the majority in whose name the new order will govern. We have no interests different from those already existing among the workers and peasants, we do not impose ourselves or our ideas from outside. The first step is the hardest – but it is the decisive one …

The train guard folded the leaflet, and looked out of his brake-van across the dusty marsh to the pottery battlements of the city, its turquoise cupolas each gleaming with a single spot of moon, like so many astronomical instruments. He told the soldier beside him: 'Some of the trains bringing supplies have been sabotaged.'

'I used to work on the railways too,' said the soldier.

'When I was young, my uncles used to say, "If you live in hope, then every day will seem different. It's foolish to be optimistic – but if you're hopeful, you'll always be interested to see what wretched thing happens next … But now I'm not hopeful: I've been round all these mulberry bushes before.'

'So you're loyal then?' asked the soldier.

'You must understand – the old sham no longer works. I'm reduced to myself: nothing uncles and soldiers say carries any weight with me. I'm just inching forward, a thought at a time: I'm being very careful with every reaction, every judgement – I've so long listened to what the station-masters and the passengers told me, "A fine run", "Late again" – I'm no longer sure I can recognise what I wanted when I went on the railways thirty years ago.

'I remember one winter we broke down with a load of horses: three weeks we were stranded, and of course we ate a horse or two. We were stuck in a great silver crust of snow. We fancied we could hear the wind in the almond trees, and smell the blossom, but it was only the snow and the wolves whisking round the train.

'When we got out, we had to pay for the horses. I had the money from my brother, but that meant he couldn't buy the land he needed, and in a year or two his youngest son wasted away. How should we know we ate the most expensive horses? They were the weakest, after all. Anyway, there you are. No one was unreasonable about things: it was just bad luck. No one troubled about the horses – least of all the owner, who'd probably assumed they were dead and lost.

'But at the end of this chain there was my nephew – dead as the horses, but to no purpose – and my brother could never work or afford more land. I've had an easy life, compared to most: there's been no one who wanted to give me answers, so I've not bothered to ask the questions. But I know that every day I am abusing something in myself: I am not all that I can be, if you understand me. I am what other people say I am – but always there's something in me saying, 'No, that is not you, you are not "A fine fellow, serving the Company well for thirty years – rather slow. Can't read."' I only know that after forty years nothing I have believed has relevance to me. I've not run out of hope – I've run out of the old model, that's all.'

'If that's so,' said the soldier, 'you belong with them.' And he waved at the desert.

'Them or you?'

'I guess we're all fairly flexible these days,' said the soldier. 'But in your position I wouldn't be the first to say anything.'

The train reached the goods yard.

'A fine run,' said a shunter.

'Come on,' said the driver. 'Leave these clowns to unpack their bombs. Don't scare yourselves to death,' he shouted.

'I am ready to leave now,' Curzon told Shala.

They were watching the full stop of the focused moon move down the sextant – like a candle flame burning down the soapy alabaster.

'Disappointment is being replaced by insouciance, orientation by commitment. I can put my shoulder to the wheel of history – and not mind if it rolls back over me,' he smiled.

'That's easy to say,' said Shala. 'Though I agree – we should take the past and future under the harrow for granted.'

'And there are no mysteries left?'

'I think people have said almost everything possible about relationships between two or three people. Masses and masses, individuals and masses – these are the relationships which require all our sensibility and subtlety ... It doesn't diminish the pleasure and the necessity that we should love each other. This must not be all, though. Even with Elizabeth, even on your knees, you were striving for self-sufficiency – and I don't want to destroy that. Our affection amuses Osman, our passion makes Sadik concerned for our political stability: and I think we both privately agree that in this kind of relationship there is a solid ground of the banal. Apart from prurience, there is only literary interest in our love – and that kind of literature is dead. I love you – so what next? How can you and I transcend the little world of you and I?'

'Yes,' said Curzon, 'I seem to have knocked around rather like a statue does – never moving, but undergoing accelerated weathering tests from all kinds of despoilers. And it's true that we shouldn't claim that it is in any way unique or exclusive.'

They sat on a pile of furs – black, silver, sand – and watched a cold pale sun hang in tension with the moon. Through the pottery frets screening the observatory window they had peepholes for a 33-foot-deep cross-section of the city. At the bottom, green squirrels were scratching for nuts – acorns and pine-nuts – on broken glazed tiles. A little above, the feet of horses – black, apricot, black-speckled silver – and above them a great pack of yellow dogs.

Nearly at the top was a dump of newspapers, posters: they could read 'To the class of '55', 'Fly To—', 'Beware – human beings spread disease', 'Have you considered emigration?' From the very top window they could see an old man on a balcony sitting up in bed, playing some kind of lute, the national colours on its neck. He wore a skullcap with an ornament in silver thread of running wolves. 'I should have been the former emperor,' said the calligram embroidered on his dressing gown. Between the toes of his right foot he held a book, *How to Master the Sacred.*

'I shall be sad to leave all this,' said Curzon.

'What makes you think you can leave anything?' asked Shala. 'I'm sorry, but the silliness of my remark was no greater than yours. Do you have the strength and courage to move about? Yes, of course you have – because your reflexiveness is a form of strength: you wish to consider everything, to let nothing escape you. But there's no time. You try to do too much – but this demands a certain appetite.'

'Yes,' said Curzon, 'yes, I think I can focus that strength, and build on what there is here …'

'Why don't you wear this bracelet,' asked Shala. 'All the men of les tribus wear a bracelet of garnets like this.'

'I'd prefer to leave it with you.'

'No, you can almost pass for one of us now. Besides, the men of les tribus are intolerably vain about things like that – so you can regard it as a disguise …'

'I think not – let Osman have it.'

'I only suggested it to make your reception in the desert seem more pleasant: I'm afraid you'll get severe cultural shock.'

And when Osman gratefully accepted it, though he did not yet wear it, Curzon wondered if, after all, he would be on more secure terms in the desert than in the city. And 'I choose insecurity,' he told Shala, who smiled.

'It would take a rock to split this into words,' said a passing musician, as Shala and Curzon spent their last morning in the city together.

'What?' asked Curzon.

'The articulation, the sinews, of the music – this is so strong: it's stronger than what it holds together. To comprehend each phrase in the music, you'd need to joint the lot. It is so difficult, you see, to play in a mock foreign style, to refer by mock archaisms to a past which never existed …'

'Why do you want to do this – why develop national styles which have no nation, historic modes which have no past?'

'I think I must be reactive – I find, however, that I cannot push my own culture forward, so I must invent other cultures to embroider, to conflate. Let me explain – if you look at these things carefully, you would know I could not use the imported themes I do: my originality, such as it is, lies in being minutely original in a large number of divergent traditions, and synthesising the lot. Our music here is cosmopolitan – we have wayside circuses travelling through Turkey from the Balkans, shepherds from the South, the wireless to the North and East. So, wherever two roads cross – there is a centre. Watch any crossroads for a day, and you'll find bagpipers exchanging thoughts, two flocks bringing two pipers together, a group with a performing bear and a drummer waiting for the same bus as the village band. We have a vast underground – forever arousing, soothing, sustaining the masses.'

'But this is surely all very notional?'

'Well, today's notions are tomorrow's theories. I'm only drawing parallels.'

'You mean to put things into words we must disarticulate, even your music?'

'I don't know how you could do that. I was only making conversation. But twenty years ago a man called Zaineddin built an enormous mechanical organ in a village not far from here. It had moving figures – priests, imams, policemen, bailiffs, musicians, bus drivers, postmen, engineers – great leering, swaying figures. Up and down they went on their iron rods, their cheeks rouged, their caftans blowing up round their ears in the breeze. The organ was itself mechanical – it played the national anthem of the surrounding countries, which alone was enough to raise a storm. But it also played themes from Beethoven, it gave a commentary in an unknown language on the life of Grieg, it sang folk songs, counting songs, played stick dances, mountain calls, temple music – and round the top of the thing a motto, "Everything is translation."

'When the machinery was started, the top revolved, the figures went up and down like on a roundabout – grotesquely jolly, one arm or both outstretched to the crowd, red eyes, red jowls, red cheeks, they cavorted and plunged in a dreamy dumb-show. People come for miles around to be amused and elevated by these wooden clowns, by the musical refuse. But it was all torn down: the police pulled it down. It was an insult, they said, to culture. And so, of course, it was.'

Later, Curzon asked Shala, 'Why do all people we meet demand quite explicitly to have us consider their point of view? Why are all so disquietingly coherent, and why can I never understand the point they are making, or indeed whether there is a point – beyond their mere existence, that is – that they wish to make?'

'If it helps, I have the same difficulty. Probably you put thoughts into people's heads, and are absurdly surprised when they tell you these thoughts. Perhaps they are simply statements to be the raw material for our realism, our materialism. They are what we mean, or what we embrace, but in a more complex and less developed state. It is more reassuring to believe that, anyway.'

‘I suppose the Wurlitzer is no more odd than the machine carbine, the mosque or the security police.’

‘I’m being dragged down by common or garden fantasy,’ Curzon admitted a little later. ‘Is this what you meant, Shala, about cultural shock?’

‘You’ll find it worse in the desert. This is why we must be rigorous, stringent, about our love. It is so easy to get lost in the decoration, to change the things which depend on forces quite unknown, to try to understand phenomena which have, for our purposes, only a surface, give only a first impression. Again, it’s a question of transcending intrinsic interest …’

‘But,’ protested Curzon, ‘this implies we should know our limitations, rather than our capacity.’

‘You’re trying to do too much – you can only indicate the areas in which other people should investigate and be active later. You must always be thinking, “Meanwhile in the war being waged against les tribus …”’

‘I accept that,’ said Curzon.

Meanwhile, Osman was talking to a poet and storyteller, Buyan Khan, whom he had long known.

‘I think it’s the heat here that makes scholarship so depressing,’ Buyan Khan said. ‘It’s the hot sticky books making for sticky thoughts, the glue of the binding melting and running like a gamy treacle between the pages. One can at least keep cool in one’s thoughts. “Still-born scholastic aesthetics,” they called my critical and published writings! What would they have called the normal run of stories, I wonder – “Come tomorrow to the wedding, bring a good story, and be sure it lasts for a week. Be sure too you get the genealogy right this time – granny was quite misled by all that unintentional incest last time you came" – that's the sort of message I get.'

'But you must tell me, how is your work again?'

'Which work?'

'How are Sadik and Shala and Curzon? How is your poetry?'

'All are splendid – but as you know, one of those could not deteriorate without the others doing so too. Does everyone know about us?'

'Well,' said Buyan Khan, 'everyone knows something: some people know all the details, but are convinced they must be mistaken. Others think it must be a joke. Some are afraid to think about it because the market rates for informers have fallen, others because the whole affair is beyond them. The police half want an insurrection to frighten the ministers, and the army would love an insurrection to make the police look foolish. So you're merrily ducking beneath the blows, while the police and the army fight it out as to who is to stage a coup. Some of the army officers are already talking with the police and militia officers to work out a joint plan – and of course you're too small to worry about.'

'But they can't play about like that! They must be fully extended in the desert – and they've to rely on drafted peasants and workers who hate and fear the feudal nonsense their officers tell them, and who are suffering acute economic distress in civilian life,' said Osman.

'If I were you, I'd be grateful for errors like that.'

'One expects them, of course – if only to balance some of one's own: but it's always a nice surprise when something you've predicted comes along.'

'When you go into the desert – and you must, sooner or later – how will you do?'

'I think,' said Osman, 'it will be a purgatory, in every possible way. The physical dangers will be relatively mild – that is, they'll be a prevision if what you in the city will have to put up with more or less permanently, if we're unsuccessful in the desert …'

'I rather doubt that Shala will be all right out there – so how about the rest of you?'

'You could come and see. "The apotheosis of Osman, poet and stevedore", "The heroic death of Curzon Khan", "The sentimental realists – Shala and Curzon" – these would make good additions to your repertoire, though they may be rather short.'

'Well, I'm pleased to think you can spare a thought for my position. If you win, what grand place in the new order will the market storyteller have? And if you lose, how bitter will the stories be?'

'You can't balance things like that: all you'll get if we win will be the chance not to be afraid. If you go on being afraid, I'd suspect that's your temperament. I'll know you were a philistine all along,' said Osman.

'You're right, of course. I must not want to live in the old way under a new mode. As you imply, there must be new things to celebrate. But it's also true that I'm afraid my technique can't be adapted to new conditions.'

'That never bothered me,' replied Osman. 'Perhaps it should have done. I just stand and watch things happen, so far as technique goes. I think that must be the last of your concerns.'

A youth in blue pebble glasses selling water shouted up loudly to them, 'Hello, comrades – we are all ready!'

'It's quite incredible,' said Buyan Khan nervously, 'how openly the old shams are being discussed, and how viciously the old guard treat the people they catch.'

'And surely it's remarkable how steadfast the prisoners are? It's that which makes me happy and unhappy, both together.'

That morning one of the couriers brought Sadik a letter on onion-skin paper, the handwriting embellished and twirled with all the languorous finesses learned in midsummer classrooms.

> *Last week our brother was taken away. We were always ready to put up with things so long as the alternatives were worse – but he always said, 'How do you know?' We were told to go to a certain field, and bring a cart; we came early, and we saw them shoot him. Without a word they did it, and he too said nothing. He'd been beaten, and we could see the teeth still driven into his lips and cheeks. They must have beaten him and then shot him. Our donkey brayed like the damned. The men said, 'Take him away, show him to the neighbours. It'll save us doing it. Now you know the best way to win arguments.' And one of them said to us, 'Now you know what you have to do, if ever you win: we'll not let you get away without committing your share of atrocities. In killing your*

brother we ensure the barbarism of your revolution – barbarism multiplied ten times …'

And so we are writing to you to say, what are we to do? They gave us a sack to put him in, and we took him home on the cart with all the dogs in the city running behind, crazy with greed. What are we to do? He'd done so little: we'd never bothered about all this. We're all human beings, I said, even though there was some as didn't worry too much about our feelings. But now, the question becomes ever more pressing – what are we to do?'

I suppose, thought Sadik, that the end of illusion is a good place to start: but explanations which take several years have always to be compressed into twenty minutes. One feels somehow that one's own total commitment absolves from responsibility for the working out of the processes. Perhaps if this were so, I should act more effectively. But if our case is on the partiality of their morality, then my feelings of greater responsibility are justified – and an increasing liability. It's nonsense to be squeamish now: but in a sense there was more hope in the hopelessness of the years in the port. Now that are we face to face with the concrete forces, we too are losing our illusions …

Curzon and Shala, however, had been discussing the possibility of writing a novel in which not only did the characters make wrong judgements about each other and act upon them, but the author did so as well.

'If you do it on purpose,' said Curzon, 'it rather loses its point, because you would rely on a certain response from your audience which to some extent you would have to elicit: the aspect of “false information” would become irrelevant. If you are just not capable of accurate judgements about your characters, this would reflect on them rather than on you, I’m afraid.’

‘You’re very prosaic today,’ said Shala. ‘I promise you that when we get to les tribus you’ll cling to any fantasy you can. We’ve lived well here: there has been time for argument, for tenderness. You and Sadik and Osman have built a little community and remained at its centre. The meetings, the discussions and the writing of programmes and pamphlets – all this now becomes secondary …’

‘But not the *tendresse*?’ asked Curzon.

‘I’m afraid not,’ said Shala, ‘though it would be better if it did.’

As they prepared to move from the observatory, the sky and the desert seemed to have coalesced in a dense band of coppery dust. Only as the light faded did the buildings and crenellations recover their outlines, a few weak electric lights warming the edges of courtyards and parks. A sign ‘Here’ flickered outside a clinic offering castration to those with sexual problems. A loudspeaker said, ‘We rely on the good sense and forbearance of the apathetic to ensure progress and stability.’ Only in the railway sidings where some labourers were playing dice, could they see human beings, quarrelling and laughing hugely. Three official cars drove up to the police barracks, sniffing at the gateway like dogs, before wheeling off to follow the trail of the desert road.

The nocturnal empire in the observatory’s cupola began to search for the thicker darknesses. Mules laden with rifles, automatic weapons and ammunition began, incautiously, to stamp and rattle down the paths on the outskirts of the city.

'I've always believed that after ignoring other people's peculiarities and excesses: on the one occasion I need to make a bit of noise myself I would be tolerated,' said Osman.

'I think certainly one can rely on the indifference of one's friends, but not of strangers,' said Curzon.

'Whatever we can't take, we must distribute now to the cadres in the city – and hope they'll do what we tell them …' whispered Sadik.

'I suppose there's nothing which isn't improvisation,' said Osman, 'but surely this kind of apportionment should have been decided earlier? But I suppose our fate is as likely to be fixed by the shouting of the mules as by our understanding of the guerrilla manuals.'

'Perhaps,' said Sadik, 'if you had not been away reminiscing, singing, drinking, rather more precision would have been possible.'

'It was essential that I demonstrate my humanity to the largest possible audience,' replied Osman.

Getting from one place to another is not so hard, it's the longueurs before you go and when you get there, thought Curzon. So here we are again – another waiting room, another terminus, another load of lethal baggage. And Shala holds the ticket, Osman has that curious bracelet which works as who knows what certificate, *laisser passer*, letter of credit, and only Sadik can read the timetable …

And he recalled the friend who had once told him, 'Since you can't be wholly selfish, in your condition the only answer is complete unselfishness.' That sounds thoroughly banal and partial, he thought – but at least there's no drink problem in the desert. He saw approaching the observatory a drunk, flames in his eyes, bitter brandy like petrol still running from his mouth. Good, thought Curzon, it's one of these evenings – and then, how inescapably trivial I am…

'Not a guard in the city who's not raving with drink,' said the drunk briskly. 'Me too, when this lot takes fire properly…'

Shala was thinking of all the dreary decades of childhood, taken to the mausolea, the 'places of pilgrimage', whose earthy morbidity cured even her austere father of his love of death. They would sit on the ground, watching the attendants sprinkling water on the night-scented shrubs, the butterflies like blots of rust on the ferrous blue of cupolas and faience, while her father taught her a new alphabet, a new dialect. Sometimes, they would see a man lying in wait for the little yellow frogs with which he fed the wise crows Shala was permitted to see, but not to touch – and which she feared more than her father, more than the desert, more than the motorbus … Only with Curzon was there no fear to be conquered – 'their very own and open city', she smiled to herself.

And yet in these few hours, in these few restricted gestures ('no bathos') could there be definitive statements? It seemed absurdly hard to live up to one's historic moments. She remembered her father angrily complaining, 'At least after all the hours I put in, I should have a vision. I wouldn't make a fuss about it: I really do think, though, that I'm owed nothing less. If I were you, Shala, I'd start from a position of utter scepticism. I'm afraid my worst fears about death are well on the way to being completely confirmed …'

She was happy at the thought that there was one problem which would not concern her among les tribus. 'I know as much now as I ever shall,' she said out loud.

'I've forgotten more than I shall ever wish to know, I'm delighted to say,' answered Curzon.

They followed the mules towards the desert.

THREE

A day later Sadik said. 'This is very serious,' 'No one could call this a desert.' They had been passing through market gardens, deserted smallholdings damp with the ooze and rot of gourds, fields of vegetables entering an extravagant decadence, cereals foxed and blighted – flowers racked with goitres and diseases, animals obese, swollen and grunting as they dragged away their smashed, pulpy loot.

Occasionally they saw in the distance wooden houses, thatched with turf, sunk deep in the ground, and sometimes a thin donkey raising water, a kind of penance for summer tasks neglected.

'Desert is a measure of desolation, not desertedness,' said Osman gloomily.

'They left the harvest this year because they thought the troops would take it if it went to the towns. So when the civil administration has taken its profit from the supplies it has stored in the city, it will be faced with bread riots,' Shala told them.

This wedge of fertility stretched out for miles, gradually cut down, jostled to a point, by the desert sands and rocks. Even on the fringe, however, there was the familiar jungular smell – mounds of grapes lying where they had pulled the vines to the ground, while fierce ants fumbled the sweet globes from shoulder to shoulder. In the water courses animals gravid with fermenting mash had drowned and burst like old wineskins.

Osman tried to think of the smell of sea, oil water, ships – hot electricity and mice – and forget the cool corrupted gas rising around them. One of the men coming with them from the city said, 'Comrades, when you find a sound marrow or whatever, you find the inside has rotted away completely – only the skin is intact. In other cases the inside and the outside have been eaten away at the same rate. But nowhere, do we find the outside decaying and the inside sound. What should we make of this?'

'Nothing at all, unless you're hungry,' muttered Sadik. 'I myself have turned away from anything organic: indeed, if I could get by on rock, I'd willingly do so …'

In the distance they could see the point at which cultivation gave way to rocks, herbs, heather. Honey-buzzards peered down at the fumbling movements in the gorse, where dispirited bees continued their minute appropriation.

'"New World?"' Curzon asked Shala as they looked out across the rancid plain. In the distance they could still see the city, with its banner – what passed locally as a double-headed eagle. A deserted seminary, straw walls round a large compound, lay to one side, a vigorous damnation in ochre spread out on the walls of the administrative buildings.

'There are red and blue teapots
In my mother's house, my dear, my lily;
But I can never go back –
I am under the net, you have ensnared me,
My heart is breaking …'

sang one of their companions.

‘It seems to me,’ said Shala, ‘that since we have so little time for developing what you might call longhand relationships, we are forced to rely on the currency of recruiting songs, professional mourning, “Aiee, aiee, my eagle is off to the wars – a thorn has pierced my lips, I will go no more to the fountain of Ismail Samani, may the silver at my breast turn black, cold as my heart …”

‘Alternatively, we can develop a personal shorthand, its symbology based on the things we know about each other, the shared experience. But we are then limited in communication to those symbols for which we have agreed a value. We can only talk in code, only meet on the prepared middle ground of the cipher book, exchanging messages with great ease under difficulties and at a distance, but effectively excluding ourselves, by secrecy, from any more intimate discourse.’

‘I suspect we just want more time – the question of the language we should use has nothing to do with our capacity for communication, only with our desire to communicate. We both say, “I desire to communicate” – but that’s trivial enough. We are as close now as people can be – you want things in their double aspect but their double aspect differentiated. You want a private language which is distinct from and more developed than, the public language which has committed us to the desert.

‘There is no such language. You are moving about uneasily in your commitment, as we all do, but don’t expect too much, and end up with nothing. If it’s understanding you want, the worst possible way to start is by emotional commitment to one person: understanding here is incidental – or inevitable. It has nothing to do with the processes of categorisation, analysis, what have you, in which we are at present concerned.'

'I don't think I understand what you are saying,' said Shala, 'but I think you understand the assurances I want. What I can't understand is why you can't or won't give me those assurances…'

'This is a very metropolitan conversation,' said Curzon, 'and it only leads down into some sombre recess, some storehouse of deficiencies, of vestigial organs, where we can only blunder about, or where a glimmer of honesty lights up all the childish horrors. I'd prefer to put this down to an inadequate evolution, rather than insufficient childhood – we all had too much of that, after all. I think you should think of me, "Man as a proper subject of science", and I of you as "pache leili", little lily – or rose, perhaps, rose is Rosa.'

'No,' said Shala sadly, 'you are nowhere near us.'

'What? Spartacus crushed?' Curzon smiled. 'I'm using the codebook at the moment. There is a soft edge of whimsy, of "we've been here before" or rather "here we go again" to all this emotional longing for uniqueness. Intellectually, I know we're not unique, and it would appal me if we were. We're not unique, Shala – there's nothing new to be said. But we are specific – can't you enjoy specificity? Make the most of your historic moment – there isn't any other kind. Make what you can of your consciousness, but don't pretend it's immortal – and don't distrust it.'

'You're getting closer, after all,' said Shala.

They passed one of the immense dance floors of baked earth, where the peasants used to bring their covered carts, the elderly watching impassively as the young people circled in mock defiance of their landlords, stamping fiercely and calling for vengeance until they were exhausted. Under the bushes they saw a few green hats, some orange feathers, some tinsel sacred hearts.

'That was as far as the missionaries got,' said Shala. 'So we never suffered from that particular run of progress …'

'There seems to have been some sort of clearance here,' said Curzon. 'Here are all the barrel staves, petrol-can shacks, astrologers' booths, screws of waxed paper for evil-eye charms, spent firework cases – and now nothing, no people, no information. Everyone has been packed up and sent off to be lost in the post: no return address. When the post office has amassed enough letters to an imaginary town, the government builds it, fills it with the dispossessed, everyone lost or delayed in transit. They'll be people stripped of their efficacy, but they'll have a massive consciousness, I suppose, which they'll never disclose …'

After all, thought Shala, it must be enough to find someone with whom I need this deep involvement, even if I can't imagine, except in the most banal and bathetically congruent terms, what forms that involvement would take. And she went on to think of her father who, towards the end of a ludicrously self-disciplined, or self-regarding life, was embarrassed by the knowledge that he could fly long distances in his sleep. After sixty years of profound conviction that his prospective actions were rigidly censored, inspected and left to mature under the most rigorous conditions, he discovered he could fly like a robot.

Despite the self-criticism, the self-destructive judgements passed by himself on his most trivial statements which allowed him a merciless critique of others, he developed this uncontrollable potential. Impossible to explain that this was the merest prelude to death, for he could permit himself to die – indeed, longed for death as a time to relax from the harrowing business of setting unattainable standards for himself and his friends – but he could not permit himself any physical or mental symptom of disease.

He had to control even the freefall of his blood pressure, swooping grimly on the high wire of his rudderless metabolism, he kept a double handful of self-control till he died of a surfeit of analogies and a rupture of the will. 'He gave himself a hard ride – always' was his chosen epitaph: he insisted on being buried outside the graveyard, among the horses and strangers. 'I'm not worthy, despite my fifty years of pilgrimage, to be buried with the faithful – and neither are the faithful,' he used to say.

And Curzon reflected that perhaps their tenderness must spring from their shared velocity as well as their common destination.

'Let us forget to be morbid,' said Curzon.

'Never too soon,' Shala replied.

'I'm convinced,' said Osman, 'that revolutionary leaders of the second quality, like us – the *faute de mieux* of the maquis, as it were – we should fade away at the revolution itself. I can't imagine schoolchildren being brought to admire our all too salient human nature – and I seem to remember Lenin saying that if the private lives of revolutionaries are to be exposed by their enemies, then they must be accurately exposed. They'd only need to talk to us, and out would rush our hopes and fears – every coin makes the jackpot.

'We're a living tribute to the ordinary and the normal, and as such a living reproach to all those who couldn't make the simplest calculation, couldn't see beyond the tip of the nearest policeman's index finger. No one, for the sake of their conscience, can afford to have us around, ageing gracelessly, quarrelling, writing waspish letters to the veterans' newspapers. It has to be the next generation which brings out into the open our quarrels and differences of objective, and is duly despised by the people who still advise us.'

'I think it's quite clear that as soon as we move away from a social base, we get soft and sentimental,' said Sadik. 'There are no people here at all, and at once we start questioning things which were long since settled. Curzon and Shala only doubt each other when there's no alternative to each other's company, and Osman tries to pre-empt the future only when there is effectively no present. I suggest we try to contact some kind of community as soon as possible…'

'Yes,' said Osman, 'there's nothing like meeting strangers for giving one the illusion that one has interesting friends. Come off it, Sadik, you can't afford to be gentle with us. It takes at least a polemic before we pay attention. Customary insults and chiding, these just signify. We're deafened by the concussion of heavier guns than you'll find in the drawing-room. One of us must be downright unpleasant: it can't be me, almost by definition. Shala and Curzon are playing hide-and-seek with their soft centres, so it's up to you, Sadik, to emerge as the cutting edge. Don't worry – you can rely on us to expose even your sham: indeed, I imagine we'd do that first.'

Sadik laughed. 'I think when we're picking martyrs, it's the quality of the last words which matter. It's between you and Curzon …'

Shortly afterwards they came upon the ruins of a city: a few ripple walls remained along with some monumental inscriptions. 'Especially magnificent in defeat, King – extends his magnanimity even to the visitors …' 'The gods even think about slaves' and 'The gods too have slaves'.

Beneath this shattered superstructure there lay a network of passages, cellars, dungeons and cheese stores. Part was still inhabited. They came upon a quarter decorated with a wild eroticism, vigorous but reflective. The proceedings were watched over by patriarchs whose beards were carefully sprinkled with the same black Greek crosses as their vestments.

'Are they in disguise, or is that simply excess of sanctity?' asked Osman. 'I suppose in this, as in so many things, we must take the thought for the deed.'

'It really does seem the work of a *nation trouvée*: how extremely difficult to excise sexual nationalism – especially when it is represented as beautifully as this,' he continued.

'Yes, aren't they silly? I don't know what they can have been thinking of,' said a woman behind them. She was one of the straitened bourgeoisie living behind a panel in the frieze. 'But at least they knew how to behave – what was nice and what was not.'

'Well, they certainly seem to have given thought to the matter,' said Curzon. 'But Otto Bauer said, "If you live in a hole in the ground, people will, *quite accidentally*, fall in on you. Much better live out in the open …" Why live here?'

'But it's ours!' said the woman. 'In the days of our hegemony, we all had places like this – only we now, for mortification, have to live in the servants' quarters.'

'Hegemony?' exclaimed Osman. 'You'll have to do better than that. In any case, there's nothing left but these passageways, so you can't introduce an element of planning into the matter.'

'When I was young,' said the woman, 'we were the most respected of the pan-Slav families in the town. We at least had ideals – and a practice which could draw together the disorganised and the oppressed. You may say this was all nebulous, that we were patronising even, that we neglected the vast mass of the population – but we did what little we could…'

'But there are no Slavs for hundreds of miles,' said Sadik.

'Well, of course that's true. That was, if you like, the natural limitation to our effectiveness. But we brought investment – our hands could lie on the roof of the factory out of work time, and we charged them nothing. We opened the "Bell-wether school for the children of foremen and overseers" – and whatever your criticism, I assure you, we were all there was. There was nothing better than us, and we have our position now because of our vision, our place in the forefront. You proletarians – what have you done? Where are your schools? You've existed in this country for sixty years, and for half a century there's been what you call a workers' state in existence. And where are you? Just dropping in to gape at the erotic frescoes, trying to mobilise a majority whose achievements so far have been ludicrous. If you sneer at me, remember you're really mocking your own feeble efforts.'

'Things may work like that,' said Osman, 'in which case you must draw what compensation you can for your own discomfort from the sight of our inefficiency. But if you'd just read some of the literature, think about things a little, consider what were the real foundations of your hegemony, you may understand our polemic as well as our analysis. I must say, though, that it's really too late to start arguing down here: after all, the arguments have been available to you for a hundred years, and if you don't accept them now, you never will.'

'But if I do accept them, what then?' she asked. 'How can I enjoy being stuck down here? I'm only mortified when I'm seen to be mortified: otherwise, there's nothing but watching these fantasies on the wall, listening to the wireless, and hoping to hear either that the government has killed several thousand agitators, or that social goodwill is flourishing. But this is poor fare: we'll not get fat on this mixture. Just once more – sell me the social revolution …'

'I really don't think you're nice enough, my dear,' said Osman.

And Shala thought of the Russian girl's diary, pleading not for a conviction but for something she wanted, needed, but could never have, and could never understand. But at least the girl had been articulate, at least she lived above-ground, watching the white moonlight on the white lilac, and the smoky fires on the stubble fields, the fool pedalling his barrel down the rutted lane to the village. Her eroticism had not been a test of endurance, no grand old trouper she.

They gloomily left the city. 'Things here seem rather worse than they did in Austria,' said Curzon. 'We seem to be sliding back all the time: it's going to be harder here than it was in the city. Can we really be convinced that dispossessed peasants on the run are going to act as an advanced class?'

'I never said that,' said Shala, 'and in any case, that argument is over. We've reached the conclusion which puts us here: I think with les tribus everything will indeed be very tough. Some of us will be broken, and others hardened – I think Curzon and Osman and Sadik will flourish out here.'

'And is that the point?' asked Osman. 'I cannot sufficiently express my contempt and disillusion if that is why we've come out here. Surely we're not here to become anything of interest to ourselves or other people?'

'You mustn't take me so literally,' said Shala. 'This is just a low point. We're cutting through the dead layers, however, even out here. And when you see les tribus, you'll know that here is the decisive point, this is the spot where the decisive steps will be taken.'

'I'm not convinced,' said Osman. 'When I was organising for the stevedores, a man said, 'Yes, I'll join the union – men will indeed be like gods …'

'And I said, "Does that mean I shall have to appear to you in a vision to collect your dues?"

'Of course things are complicated, and we're complicated with them. Of course our perception will be sharpened by the time in the desert. But if I wanted to sharpen my perception I'd sit by a lake and write ghazals. Now, what sort of shape are we in to meet les tribus? Can we really claim to offer participation, let alone leadership?'

But mysteriously, although each was convinced that the others lacked understanding and an awareness of the dimensions and modes of emancipation, they went on with more determination.

'We are in transition,' Sadik reassured himself.

'I can, I must bring this tiny party to the point where it can freely and genuinely assume leadership and responsibility. In transition, you can only remember the familiar language and responses of the townsmen, and the railwaymen in particular. And we can think of what we know of les tribus. But we can't talk about our own feelings. Perhaps later Shala and Curzon can play endlessly on each other's sensibility – but not now: their responses must be of the most prosaic kind. They must be positivistic, as they think, but their positivism may indeed contain that precision, that control, we need.'

In front of them, thought it was midday, they could see the flaming gondolas and barques – the kites of les tribus.

'We must penetrate the lines tonight.'

At nightfall they came to an expanse of rubble. Fractured clay pipes brought conversations of the troops to them.

'We seem to be the heart and soul of a telephone exchange,' said Curzon.

They heard a corporal talking to a recruit: '"No type, no proclamation," the editor said. You see, the governor's decree used letters of the old alphabet, and we'd no letters in the fount. The censorship said we must print all or nothing – we couldn't change a letter. So we never printed the proclamation closing us down. And so we never had to close down!'

The recruit said, 'And yet you're here. And les tribus wouldn't trouble to ask you about the old alphabet if they caught you.'

'Well, what's your argument?'

'You've been cut off from les tribus: moreover, you're an opposite sides. Moreover, all us soldiers have been told to report any subversion. So you're three ways caught!'

'If you believe that, you're crazy as well as odious,' cut in another voice. It was as if the whole battlefield lay over a seething hypocaust.

Curzon as usual was amazed by the changes effected now by the greater fluidity and articulation of his own remarks and perceptions. It was as if he had acquired a mental viscosity in place of a crotchety desperation. Out here, people had not rejected the arguments, or decided to forget them, or found substitute satisfactions – they had simply never been told about them. Men were now for the first time meeting suggestions that their distress was fused to them by human agents.

They could hear through the pipes someone painfully translating, 'Now I have the right to salute creatures I don't know … They pass before me and gather in the distance … Though everything of this I see is strange to me … And their hope no less strong than mine …'

'An officer presumably?' said Osman.

'… *Cortèges o cortèges …*'

After some time a man from les tribus arrived. 'I've been asked to take you through the lines,' he said. 'Though all you need to do is just keep straight on. They're all much too busy playing cards and arguing about this and that to worry about us.'

'How did you know we'd be here?' asked Sadik.

'It is wrong to think the desert is deserted – it's a measure of desolation …'

'I fear the army's disorganisation will be a reflection of les tribus' dislocation and defensiveness,' said Osman.

'It looks better the other way round,' said the man. 'From the other side, that is.'

'There should always be more time to reflect,' thought Curzon. 'How can we raise ourselves from pathos when we're being led about in the dark like so many blind bulls, Mithras-Oedipus? But instead, one thought jostles another: if we stop, we find a heap of associations, jokes, lies, tumbled over us, or piles of automatic rifles falling about our ankles…'

The man from les tribus said, 'Hurry up, I was the only one who thought it would be worth our while to guide you in. The others were still arguing about what should be done, and now I'm feeling tired. It would break my mother's heart to see me now …'

'Why?' asked Osman.

'She was always anxious that I should make a good death, and make it while she was young enough to enjoy it. My survival has outlived her horror of death. She just doesn't care now. Her or me – it's all the same.'

Shala deeply regretted her eagerness to see them all in the desert. 'Have I come home? Surely not, because the signs are that we're unwelcome. Have I condemned Curzon to death – and if so, was it out of selfishness or belief that only some such confrontation could resolve our unsuitabilities? Was I simply correct at a tactical level so low that it is even now irrelevant?'

'Keep going now,' said the guide, 'and you'll soon be in amongst them. I'm going back to bed now. We have to get up much too early for my liking …'

'I remember him from the town,' said Sadik. 'He used to make the worst locoum I ever tasted – in that shack by the station. We must hope he is not the cook.'

And Osman thought, 'Aiee, but I am hurt all over. I could bellow with the pain, which is partly the pain of dragging my flayed body in and out of doorways, other people's marriages, up mountains, over deserts. There is only one, decisive struggle, and I've had forty years of it. Hold up, sad old body, aching old mind. "Spartacus crushed …?" No of course not. It would be so pleasant if there was just a little of the downhill, though …'

For the next few days they were passed back through what les tribus called the 'circles' – the fighting communities ranged in depth behind the front line, awaiting their turn in the battle.

In an atmosphere both of anti-climax and rising apprehensiveness, the small group was directed back to the political committee of les tribus. Although they passed over two hundred miles of desert, their impressions were confused.

'Les tribus don't want us,' said Osman.

A man stopped and listened.

'Yes, this is the difficult part,' said Sadik, but without hope.

'Well, "fighting masses cannot *at the very beginning* occupy the industrial centres"… "Only in the process of the further development of the revolutionary struggle can the peasant war led by the proletariat expand to new territory." We're all busy reading up the literature. 1930 they said that. Perhaps you're what we need. Perhaps … Anyway, they can't use their aeroplanes against us – they're being kept back in the capital,' the man told them.

'In some parts of the "circles" things are happening at least as quickly and inventively as among the troops. But in other "circles" people don't understand at all what is at stake – and don't even care that even now we are capable of winning victories,' he continued.

Later, Osman wrote in his diary:

> *There was mist like silk this morning. Shala and I watched the sun slide up silver – she smiled like a proud bird. How strongly drawn to her I am … A wounded lynx limped among the poppies, orange, pink, scarlet, purple poppies – remember how it growled. The Russian girl said, 'In the sheaves there are dried carnations, scraps of paper saying "Peace", "World". They're so big and heavy the women can hardly lift them …'*

'I am now merely bored by all the symptoms which once fed my egoism,' thought Curzon. 'And the symptoms are beginning to fade. But what is there left of me? I am being restored to nature piece by piece: history is reclaiming all the thoughts and sensations I borrowed. Only a petrified droplet of originality remains: it's like a cabochon – I can no longer look at the world through it. But it's all a long way from the Use of Combray …'

'There comes a time,' Shala told them, 'when we look back over what we've done, and can't see the connections. Was there a kiss of peace? Did the archbishop's horse really press him to reach a compromise in the new creed? Did the craftsmen of Golden Hero immolate themselves because they had created perfection? We don't know which are lies, which metaphor – the answers are in part questions of aesthetics.'

'It's nice to hear answers becoming questions again,' said Sadik. 'And it's nice to find Shala as devious as Curzon…'

'I would rather have Shala scrabble about and find some lapis lazuli cities, or a library. Whimsy is for cities. We're living now in the margin of our real concern: for us – it's the printing press, the manifesto. Certainly not this walking about, the strange dialects and finger-talk…' complained Osman.

Sometimes, however, they would see patrols from the flocks of wild camels, and Osman would try to join in the song their guide always sang when they saw them. The group passed through fantastic landscapes: for hours they would walk over a web of blue flowers – apparently a net over water, the stems silvery and strong. But at times when they peered down through the stalks they saw no water at all, or what looked like the corners of sandstone buildings, statues of winged animals, inscriptions always beginning 'Those who would count in years' or 'Wherein lies yesterday's news?' Once they found ruined warehouses full of the artefacts of a civilisation which had never been articulated – clothes, weapons, design – mute and unusable.

'I think this sand has a head start over the people,' said Osman, 'and all sand knows about is creeping inexorably forward. While we creep inexorably back.'

For one whole day they wound round the spirals of a pass leading from one mountain plateau to a lower – the one above red and sulphurous, the one below covered with the dark-blue earthworks of creatures like foxes, feathers from the red and grey geese which stood in the dull blue mud of the streams.

The guides were now amused, now irritated, now alarmed by the curiosities of the desert trail. Especially did they dislike the cockleshell pass, as it deepened and darkened to a skull-like green. At times they would whoop and sing: 'This water which burns my throat takes me to the dark, and I can lie down by the flagon. But there is water with fish and stars in it. Why does my love give me bitter wine, when I could be fishing – catching love for my love, and no bitterness, bitterness from the thorn…'

And sometimes they would play dice – throwing the dice, large as fists, along the path ahead, running on to pick them up. But more often they pointed out to Shala, who may have known this already, and to Osman, whose annoyance was diminishing, the dialectical features of their language and the aspirations implicit in the usage.

'Until a generation ago there were two modes of all the desert languages, a right and a left one, one for women and one for men. But the two are merging – some languages adopting the more left, others the more right, of the original modes …'

Curzon told Shala, 'I am not changed by the desert. I see nothing more clearly.'

'You are becoming more austere. You can look more firmly at some things, and ignore other things. You're less forthcoming: perhaps you're less receptive. But you must see you have a capacity for development. That's all I told you. That's all I want …'

'How admirable all that sounds,' thought Curzon.

'The problem is not how to avoid capture but how to avoid surrender – do you remember who said that, Osman?' Shala asked.

In the city they had left, the Inspector of Police told the local commander, 'Our problem is not to avoid executions, but how to keep things moving in the pipeline. It's essential to avoid mass executions and mass arrests. Decide on a normal and regular figure and stick to it …'

In the desert, Osman said, 'The last time we tried this, we only got as far as some sort of commune, some transitional state, in the port. It was all too easy. The police were frightened, and just sat there, patting their horses, and holding up the bolts of their rifles. We didn't last long enough to find out the police spies among us. I worked with Nazim – Minister of the Interior – and neither he nor I owned a pair of socks.

'History shows who wins' – that should have been our motto. We'd no chance, but even in those first days we had all the arguments about what we should do with the prisoners and so forth. Half of us were turning police stations into museums while the other half were building new ones. Half of the committee were exalted with their hunger, the other half irritated by it, and by the peculation in the department of food supply. What we did, in fact, was to start to arouse the mass of the people to grant that we had a potential and that they themselves would have some part, however small, to play. But all the corruption of the old system burst out and multiplied furiously as soon as we'd broken the crust. Or perhaps it broke through the crust of its own accord and we were just trying to control its speed …'

'But do you think the same things exist among the people here?' asked Shala.

'It's irrelevant – and there's nothing about absolution in the manifesto. I don't think anyone can tell you how les tribus will react. Their own social organisation seems still intact. I would say, as an informed guess, that things will turn out to be very various …'

Osman enjoyed his mischievous conjurer's honesty. 'You see,' he seemed to be saying, 'believe me, you're absolutely right. You're right when you see the trick. You're right when you realise it *is* a trick. You're right when you start to wonder how it's done. You can trust me – I'm not one of your dishonest or optimistic magicians who pretends there's no trick, or that there's magic beneath it all. I'll even show you the books I get the tricks from. A little thought, a little practice – put them together, and there's no mystery at all.'

'I think we sustain personality and character in all kinds of ways,' Shala said to Curzon. 'Our own, that is, and other people's. When I was young we had a postcard of the Shah mosque in Isfahan, and the green of its cupolas was the hazy dark green of those bushes, and of the uniforms of the militia sitting on the steps of the Shark Hotel. Always my mind is straining at the connections between things, and always it seems so inadequate. How annoying to reject vulgar common-sense, but be able to make no further discovery … Even to be in love falls below expectation because understanding is not deep enough to control – not deep enough even to understand

and enjoy ... Sitting here by the tents of les tribus, so much that is archaic, so many street scenes, frozen in sepia, sun-glazed, sun-hardened, sun-blind, the image fading at last from the smokey glass – lie just behind my eyes.'

'We reflect on action – and action is reflected from us,' said Curzon. 'But we know too that we may never even have half an hour when we dominate the archive in our heads. Even when we do, it may be like Osman – releasing the prisoners his own department had taken. "I saw they knew they were caught," he told me, "and I thought what an interesting situation that was. Just interesting. To shoot them – that would not be interesting. And I knew what a criminal fool I was. I'd not have done it if I'd not been too tired. In a week the positions were reversed, and we were carried off like kittens under the eyes of the men we'd failed, left standing on the sidewalks watching the police camions take us away. Each man had his hand under his coat with the dynamite or the Browning ready. Ready for twenty years, but too old now to have me say, 'After the revolution, the hard work begins ... Then we start over again.'" But I know what you mean about those photographs.'

They were in the last 'circle' before the political committee. The tents of les tribus had been goat-brown at the front, but now they were nearly black, blackened with smoke and purple dye. The men sat reading old newspapers, cannibalised trucks, made kites, or lay eating the sharp apricots and quinces which grew nearby. A young man in a yellow fur hat was writing a poem to an instrument like a shantur which lay beside him: he had a flagon of wine which smelt of jasmine. A grey cat with tufted ears swept a paw across the shantur's strings from time to time.

'What are you writing?' asked Curzon.

'That the shantur is never angry. That it has more music to it than was ever played. That what it has played it has forgotten. That I must not be angry, as the shantur is not angry. But I have a horse, I have a pass for the truck that takes me to the front. If there is no road and no horse, then I can walk. Look for nothing but a pass, a shantur, sandals worn through … do not look for my anger – but you must hear my music.'

They watched him at work for a time. 'This is only a draft,' he said.

One evening Osman inched into sleep, still half aware of the black brown white grid of the rug on the tent floor. He was back looking at just such a metal grid on a gallery in a big Moscow store, looking down into the mass on the ground floor slowly seeping round the merchandise, gathering like iron filings round the lines of force of clothing and hardware … He fell, and was back in the tent.

'I shall always be grateful to the Soviets,' he told Shala. 'They gave me asylum. But it wasn't an easy time. Not a comfortable time at all. It's hard to be underground in your own society, and it wasn't easy to pretend that it didn't matter, and that I didn't care.'

'Why, what did you see when you were asleep?' asked Shala. 'The "red fool furies of the Neva"?'

'Worse than that.'

They looked at each other, and Osman thought, 'How good to know how sweet she would be, how bitter-sweet the ending, and how good to know enough to remain at a certain distance, speculating, savouring, remembering, refining – like a man crawling through thorns to watch a lynx intent on some game with pebbles and cones. And yet – to be another lynx? But weren't there lynxes enough …?'

And it seemed to Shala that here it was better to be inarticulate – here was a relationship best conducted in mutual and confidential silence – or misunderstanding.

'If Osman is happy never quite knowing, then that is a good and decisive reason why I should be happy too on that basis,' she thought. 'It's for ever a matter of interpretation – not documents.'

*

'What should a peasant like you be doing here?' asked the guard.

'I'm not a peasant,' said the peasant. 'I've a son who's a lawyer. He takes coffee at the American Club.'

'You are a peasant,' said the guard.

'Yes, lord,' said the peasant.

'We have every intention of shooting you.'

'I did not have to be here. I have two colts the colour of strawberries. I have a ring with an amethyst – oh, as big as a colt's eye. You'd never get me to part with one of these colts. Sharp as knives, did I say? The colour of strawberries? Sure and sharp as time. The colour of blood.'

'I don't like this killing. My father was a man like you.'

‘And the ring. Who guards that, you ask? Well,’ he said, ‘where could it be? Yes, guarded by bees – we all know that. But which bees?’

‘My father could sell better than you.’

‘Yes, lord. Long life to him – and to you, lord.’

‘You’re crazy. Why not call your son?’

‘He’s dead. Shot.’

‘We will shoot you.’

‘I don’t want to die. I’m afraid.’

‘We are not yet through with killing. Perhaps we will never end. Would you shoot me?’

‘No, lord. Not me. Not myself. I know how hard it is for us peasants, and our sons. But in my village there are a score of people …’

‘“It’s a fool who fools fools,” they say where I come from,’ said the guard.

‘And we say, “He who is fooled is a fool” – so what?’

‘Give me your hat.’

It was a green felt hat with a band of fox fur.

‘Why?’

‘We never shoot people with their hats on.’

‘I am afraid to die, lord.’

‘There are twenty others.’

‘My ring will be deep in the autumn honey. No one will find it. Things are very various. But I remember: “Long live the International.”’

*

Sadik remarked to Curzon, 'Herzen said of one's relationship with a woman, "We are first intimate and then acquainted." I feel rather like that with les tribus. The peasant cart, the nomad's tent – heaving away at them when all the time the mule is harnessed to the side we can't see, all ready to move off and leave us in the mud.

'Your Otto Bauer once said, "Out of politeness we may affect to be amused by another's mild eccentricity. What must really concern us is whether he can shed his madness in the new society." I find it so difficult to decide what we should import, what will continue despite our efforts, and what we should be attempting to destroy in the relations of les tribus. At the meeting with their political committee we must present ourselves as experts only on urban affairs. And yet we are at the mercy of the couriers here. Just as, in the desert, we rely entirely on les tribus. This is very healthy, as it should be: but it makes for anxiety …'

They had at last reached the political committee, in the centre of the 'circles'. However, the 'circles' were shrinking: the front was approaching, and the loose organisation of les tribus was being welded, willy-nilly, into a single fighting force. The pressure of events was bringing the political committee too into a position of greater significance.

The meeting was to take place in a sand-silted cupola, open to the sky. Already three musicians, who would play throughout the proceedings, were beginning the early morning music, irritatedly changing from 'right' to 'left' modes as now men, now women, came to change seating arrangements.

For several hours the members of the committee declared their interests and explained their precise powers and intentions. But there were so many archaisms and so many bursts of delighted laughter and remonstration at unexpected shifts of position or acquisition of influence, that Sadik found it hard to follow.

Allandur, to whom the chairmanship had rotated, said, 'The sea, the sea, always reconstituted. Gul-ei here holds away over certain concepts. We have decided that it shall be for him to propose definitions over these concepts: to decide how many squares, as it were, the game shall be played over. Dzhulga has the interest over logistics: he provides you with reference points in materiel. Kul-Sarayev, he has brothers in the Soviets. He will perhaps be able to interpret our positions in terms you can understand …'

Osman explained to Curzon, 'They have tried to intellectualise a political structure which really does not exist. But beneath the familial forms they perceive ideological forms. As yet there are really no ideological conflicts. Everything we need to know about their beliefs and interests is open – we simply have to join it up in a pattern which makes sense to us.'

'But how can it?' asked Curzon. 'Otto Bauer always said that one needed a language so concrete that one could present demands and make appeals without touching the existing ideological defences of the audience – but that he himself was not clever enough to devise it. Let's hope les tribus have discovered it themselves.'

Allandur continued, 'We even have a local form of the dialectic. But we are all unsure of its application. We would respect its successful user. I fear we are not prepared to approach the problem “scientifically”.’ He laughed, ‘Our science is the science of artillery and gas. We need the dialectic – but suspect it is in the hands of our enemies.’

Gul-ei said, ‘In the towns you must be at war with all objects, with all the things you have made, or almost all. We have a more complex relationship to the things we find around us, even the ruins of cities and technologies which lie beneath our feet. Things have not only many uses, but many appearances, calling for a greater sensibility. Only, we don’t have the vocabulary. We can hardly tell each other how beautiful we are, or how tormented.’

‘But this is also my problem,’ said Osman.

‘Then we are at least a little way towards beginning,’ said Gul-ei. ‘You are intelligent people, and you run ahead of the simple mechanics of time. I need not explain to you how far we have got today. This has all been most successful. The music is becoming exciting – I suggest we concentrate on that for the rest of the day.’

‘Not a moment too soon,’ muttered one of the musicians. ‘We’ve finished morning, flowers and animals while you’ve been talking. Though I prefer afternoons, fountains, drinking, women, there is a naivety about the morning which people never appreciate.’

‘The first scale to make them laugh, the second to make them cry, the third to send them to sleep. Yes, after all, how could one hope to do more – expect perhaps to change the order.’

The musician had started playing at dawn because, he explained to himself, ‘no one ever hears the dawn music’. But no one heard it then, and when he had finished, the man said, 'After all, perhaps I'm just crazy about music.'

Already there was excitement at the arrival of Sadik and the others. 'Who have come from Moscow to tell us how to win,' while others said they were not Russians but Chinese, or Roumans. And others said, 'They have no country. They are like us.'

But in fact many of les tribus had seen Shala in the city, and knew very well what the discussions were to cover. 'We have a great capacity to turn even our destiny into myth,' said some.

> *The peasants sing and dance as they go to the fields,* [said the Russian girl's diary], *but oh how tired they are in the evenings … Bloody from the claws of the sheaves, racked with – can it be vodka? But the manager said he wouldn't let them drink in the fields. And these summer fields are so dry, the dust flies like sparks, sparks among the sheaves: and the peasants are so strong … Today I drank vodka on the terrace till the white railings bent and bowed, and the paths flickered like the tongues of lizards, bees searching for sweetness, and the whole day turned to gold, round gold, roundels of gold like a pile of gold coins spilling and rolling …*

In the desert, people were alarmed at the harshness of the morning. The music came from the shattered dome with a metallic clarity. Gule-ei looked at the circles of men in silver and green caftans squatting in the shade of the cracked pottery walls. He listened to the clattering of the dutar and the intense instructions given by its master, to the men discussing the music, their Brownings, a horse.

'Perhaps we shall survive,' he thought. 'If only because we've built no walls, no cupolas. We can ride away, over the desolation, as far as our energy takes us. Hunting in the morning, music in the afternoon, writing books in the evening – can it be like that when the napalm comes? Is it really like that now? Are we really even now free without our polyclinics? Is Sadik right, that we have feudalism with lords, that we are persecuted by the government because it is too afraid to persecute its day labourers – and are the day labourers stronger than we?' And he thought, 'I did not mean to keep people in ignorance of their potential – but have I not done so?'

'Perhaps,' thought Gul-ei, 'the austerity which we prize sets like cement, and inhibits emotion. We always think our splendid and allusive philosophy hovers on the verge of crystallisation, that it is always in full flight, the "process of the formation of a collective will".'

Without a bright tear in his eye, he imagined the building of his ideas crumble. Now that he was outside, he could see the barred windows – the concepts were cells: the reasonings and the arguments – the corridors of a prison.

'I go over to the other side,' he told his comrades. 'I cannot yet tell you why, but there are problems which we cannot perceive using our present methods.'

Allandur remarked, 'This becomes very difficult. We can easily enough replace Gul-ei, but we would have first to account for his defection. Myself, I think he has taken a step which we might all need to take. We can produce a machinery of coercion from what is left of our philosophy – easy. But then I could not continue to defend it in the same terms – it would have ceased to emancipate, let alone to enable us to understand.'

'I reached my present position,' added Gul-ei, 'through the rigorous application of our own method …'

Kul-Sarayev was thinking that significant changes really could not take place in this way. But then, it was always the incongruous and the unsuitable who were found in the front line, against their judgement and expectation. If there was to be a front line at all, one must accept the front line as it was.

'I should like,' he said, 'to have a talk with my brothers in the Soviets.'

'How long will that take?' asked Osman.

'Perhaps for ever – for the talking. Perhaps never, because, as you know, we cannot correspond. I make the point only to show you what I would like to happen – and to show too that we no longer have the choice.'

'Otto Bauer described a similar situation,' said Curzon. The musicians came forward, since Bauer had a local and undeserved reputation as a lover of music.

'He said that the ideas which are the most abrasive are the best. Old ideologies sink down through society and are made brutal by the ill-will and frustration of their users: but always there are sad people who are attached to these ideas – ideas of savagery, of paradox, of people who do not recognise themselves, who wish themselves dead to quieten the rattling of irreconcilable beliefs, actions, aspirations. You cannot help these people, he said. Nor can you, at such a stage, decide whether you fight – if you must fight – or die, if you must die.

You choose – and then within strict limits – only whether you win or lose. And there I cannot help you.'

'That sounds like nonsense,' angrily shouted the man with the dutar. 'Let him say what he means. Which ideology? Which lords? Who fights who? Enough of this disappointed Bauer man. All those doubts and discriminations are made, to give an example, in the music for the late afternoon. But it's a busy time, and no one much bothers about it.'

'That sounds a fair criticism,' thought Shala. 'I think the time has come to drop Bauer.'

'I feel Bauer is too heavy a piece of baggage for us,' agreed Dzhulga. 'Try not to be so devious, Curzon. You're writing the history of the movement before it even exists. We've all read Bauer, and conceivably rejected him for reasons better than yours for swallowing him whole.'

'How did you know Bauer's work?' asked Curzon.

'You underestimate Shala,' said Allandur. 'I suspect you underestimate most people. But don't worry. We can't expect that we shall be attractive versions of the people we hope will be developed long after our death …'

They discussed matters for three more days. At times the musicians would tire, and come over to the committee to give advice. They passed through boredom, excitement: they broke off to watch a flight of eagles, very fast, very high, blown across the sky like the scraps of newspaper blown across the sand – scraps tiny with attrition saying only 'defection', 'two kopeks', 'founded by V.I. Lenin in 1912'.

Osman surreptitiously read the Russian girl's diary:

> *when all the vodka was gone, it began to rain. I ran out into the garden and the drops pressed on my face like cool metal, and the sheaves smelt of the fur of mice. I could see the trees, miles of red, gold, black trees, smelling like caraway vodka, and all round the golden dust darkening, mottling …*

'Osman! How long since we saw the last courier?' asked Sadik.

'Six days. But they are probably delivering messages to the "circles" who cannot pass them back here. It would be easy to establish our links again, if les tribus will agree to cooperate, and coordinate …'

Now, he thought, in the big cool warehouses at the port, the men will be waiting for the heat to subside. They will have the bottles and the dice: the scent of carnations will be coming off the sea. They will be singing 'Vingt Ans', they will be singing 'Little Lily'. How good to sit there, very quietly, peacefully: bread, melons, sunflower seeds. The humble expeditions to the lakes, the harsh deserts, a life passed very close to the ground, but replete with tiny acts of self-indulgence, every privation sweetened with a drop of contemplation and speculation. Thirty years of nothing in particular …

In the city, the police had ceased justifying themselves. Interrogation had become a dreary routine. The officers became more boring, in the eyes of their wives, and refused violin lessons to their little daughters, candy-bowed and petulant. Coercion became a sweated industry.

'We'll give them some standards they'll not match,' said a lieutenant. 'I've stopped worrying about security – it's numbers I'm after.'

And the organisation Sadik had left in the city grumbled that indiscriminate arrests made it hard to recruit. 'Why don't they spend a little time and trouble, finding who are the important ones?'

The writers' clubs were closed: the university taught only law and engineering, and the people's music concerts in the parks were deserted. Food was allocated to the city poor, to prevent subversion. But with their new strength they developed a huge black market, thriving on sabotage, blackmail and theft. Soldiers who would not desert to les tribus deserted to the ragged entrepreneurs and captains of finance in their tin shacks under the walls.

Stories of atrocities ran round the city's bars: 'Both sides are wrong,' sadly enthused the speculators and the social lions.

Meanwhile, in the forward areas the soldiers continued to unmask the security services. 'It is essential,' said a corporal, 'that we should know precisely where everyone's interests and sympathies lie.'

'But that would be politics,' said another.

'Not at all. We common conscripts just stand together against the officers and against the government. That's not politics. All we need to know is: who will let us home earlier.'

'It's not easy to fit an affair into the interstices of a revolutionary war,' said Curzon.

'Don't worry,' replied Shala, 'we will have plenty of time, or none. No one is bothered about us. I am taking everything in – especially the unspoken bits. There's no shortage of pathos and *tendresse*, no lack of the great metropolitan emotions, if that worries you. You don't need time now to explain yourself:

this is a period when your campaign diary tells me more about you than ten tedious winters spent together on the top of the stove.'

'I can turn "what is" to good advantage – but I can never quite be reconciled to the fact that what is is all there is. I remember – thousands of fish stranded on the shore, waiting on the hope that the largest wave had not gone for ever …'

They moved out through the circles once more, towards the front. Now, people would stop them, tell them what was happening in the city. The group, accompanied by the political committee, crossed plains, deserts, mountain ridges, which made Curzon feel that every conceivable quirk of memory, of fantasy and optical illusion, had been taken out of the inside of his head and constructed, ten times life size, from the most bizarre materials.

On one day's march they would find yesterday's customs become today's eccentricity. Musical instruments would be blown in one village and used as percussion in the next. There were even cities – though without roads leading in or out, where a few hundred people knew only the space within the crumbling walls and collapsed gateways. Slowly reading through the imperial libraries, picking off the glazed tile alphabets and sparrows from the walls of the equestrian school to serve as plates and decorations, these men grew food in the gardens of their dead neighbours. They reared huge mushrooms in the forsaken houses, leaving them to dry in the sun, like saddles, in the streets.

'We feel rather left out of everything,' they said. 'Having once been an imperial people, and this a provincial capital, when the whole thing withers away, there hardly seems any point in starting all over again. Besides, we've only got the old stock of ideas to work on – and we know where they lead: they lead to us!'

At times they rattled across immense grassy plains – broken by a clump of sunflowers, a wallow for some thin cows, a wooden watchtower for spying on the sheep, here and there a herdsmen lifting his broad felt hat to them as they passed.

'You must realise,' said Allandur to Sadik, 'that however staid we may appear to you, we have accomplished our own minor revolution. We have khans even now sitting in the Cuban bars of the major hotels, eager to see us destroyed and handed back, with full mineral and prospecting rights, embalmed to them. Who ever heard of primitive peasants overthrowing their khans and appointing a political committee? Well, here we are. To hell with khans! Here we are, making our first unaided appearance. We can show we have a real social force, a political presence …' He stared at Sadik.

'This has been worrying me,' said Sadik. 'I know we can make something of les tribus: militarily, yes, you have been crystallised – and created – by the pressures on you, which in turn reflect the impossible task of containing you, ignoring you, within the existing system. But are you not socially still the weakest link? If we bring in the day labourers, the conscripts, the workers – will you not then have to endure a process of social transformation?

'Of course, we would all like to say "carry on in the old way – but without want, without oppression". But how is this possible? Under the old way, you had no chance of deciding your own future – now you have such a chance, you have won it – if you like, you have won the right through the eloquence of your rifle-barrels.

'But it may be a right only to pronounce your own sentence of death. Death, that is, as you see it: when you are fighting like this, all kinds of things appear possible. The most fantastic suspensions and distortions of concrete forces – which do indeed occur on the battlefield – seem possible as a permanent condition.

'We should try to master the processes whereby this indeed is possible. But it is not yet possible. Your strength is derived from your being poor, rootless, oppressed, neglected: your strength comes from the creativity of your reaction to this condition, which you are trying to end. Your victory will free you from want, but your poverty provides the foundation for your heroism.

'This is not a riddle, not a paradox: it is something you must accept and prepare people for, and in time, turn to good advantage. Do not become a prisoner of the past from which even now you are trying to break free …'

And Gul-ei thought, 'So to break out of the old way of thinking was a mockery of liberation. In my head I am free, but my body is still the slave to necessity. To look over these plains, seeing them covered with bee-hives, foals, apricot trees, polyclinics, technical institutes – this is impossible. In the desert, the underground libraries are burning. We have been reduced overnight to one language, and there is no longer time to invent names for new concepts. We must make do with what we have, with what we can remember … But will this satisfy Shala?'

'It is all becoming crushingly austere,' Shala told Curzon. 'The discussions in the observatory, Osman's lies – this now stands at the end of a long perspective. Even though I love you, it seems to matter less. It is a precondition of being able to manage each day's march, to speak and write for les tribus, to piece together the reports of the couriers. Without it – perhaps I could not continue – but that is not important for itself.

'Everything in the past seems eclectic. We no longer need to sift through alien cultures, rescuing a few shards, gestures, customs. We have now our own precision, our own concreteness. My love for you doesn't now distort me, nor do I have to distort my love. It is worth exactly what it is worth: it doesn't dominate me, or warp my judgement. It is as natural to me as literacy or good eyesight ...but possibly I'm still confused?'

'I'm a much poorer specimen than you,' said Curzon. 'I think I agree with you – on average. But my average is reached from wild extremes. Sometimes I am rubbed away to a shred of the collective consciousness, capillary. But I don't think your hardness is austerity. It's just a sign that the speculation has to be put aside for the moment. We've stopped being archivists, we've stopped working in the margins of other people's lives...'

In a bar in the city a corporal was talking to some conscripts: he was drinking thin brown wine, made from the slender early grapes, and the table in front of him was sticky, as if with pomegranates.

'Out there, we're saying, "Here is the rose. And here we must dance!" What? Spartacus crushed? We're all fine and ready. Two steps forward, three steps back? No, no more of that … Rats in high collars, that's all they are …'

'Who?'

'Officers, gentlemen … why, there's lads in my company who'll tell you everything there is to know about today … This is the last gentleman's war I fight. Next time, we'll see what kind of show the khans put up on their own. I'm so tired... Fighting our own … what can that do?'

He poured down more and more of the wine. 'Scarlet roses … purple roses … black roses, cobalt roses … smell of enclosed sun … the honey melts and the bees still sweat to the hive … On the rock – but we'll have the officers before the end of the month.'

He tilted his head back, and watched miles of inner space unravel, streaming past, flickering like grass stems.

'Yes,' said his audience, 'we know all about it, comrade. But you must be patient, you must not doubt your capacity for surviving the transition …'

'This is only one chronicle of our revolution,' Gul-ei wrote. 'I do not hope to do more than show some of the knots on the underside of the carpet, which hold the design in place… Many of us see no design – some see no carpet. I was born in a lighthouse. My father was the keeper – and the post was a sinecure. We grazed goats on the shoals on the lake bed – the water had long ago dried up, run off in earthquakes. My father was often mocked about this.

'"Well," he would say, "if the water comes back, I shall be at once occupied – and safe," and perhaps I have learnt that lesson, the only one he taught me.

'We had khans for only forty years … we were nomadic for only twenty years. Yet in that time we have come to appreciate the social and cultural sources of our cohesion. It has been possible to take the least accomplished, the most vulnerable peasants, and set them to wander about the countryside, and by the very enforcement of hardship make them capable of resistance and great feats of imagination.'

He broke off and watched the green-grey-white smoke rising from the twig fires where the day's first coffee was being made. On the horizon, thin black smoke rose from lorries ambushed before dawn.

'Already,' he thought, 'I feel I have said all there is time for. To continue would not only be pretentious – it would contradict our collective needs …' He did not entirely understand this. He remembered the song his father used to sing:

My komuz is made of cherrywood:
I love it, and have followed its melodies
Over the desert and into the mountains.
But now, I play it in the orchard,
For we are a peaceful people.
And would live peacefully.

'He couldn't say that now,' said Gul-ei, half aloud. His thoughts were hard, dry, thin: Perhaps because I am old, perhaps because I understand, he thought.

As an afterthought, he wrote: 'Shala – has she misled Curzon? She is just too preoccupied to remember how strange this all is to him: what use here can he hope to be? What has he to give? Sadik and Osman, they may not draw les tribus to them but they represent the best there is. They are men like the leaders of the day labourers, the railwaymen, the soldiers. And they have understanding – and Osman a talent. But not Curzon? A talent for contemplation?'

Already more councils of revolutionary soldiers had been formed. Some whole regiments were refusing to move forward or back. A document was being circulated called, 'Some new definitions of democracy and popular power.'

All round now was an expanse of cinders, rags, oil, soot. 'Here is the rose,' whispered Osman to himself, 'and here we must dance.' The front was held by a thin line of les tribus, but there was no firing.

The Russian girl's diary spoke of her visit to the village:

Where, long, long after my death, long after I have been burnt away – like the little pine church here which burnt down one night, so that the priest couldn't tell where it had stood, among all the ash left by the woodcutters – no one will have to destroy themselves, as I have done. The vodka burns – but the rain is so cool … The gold is cool too, but the gold begins the fire …

Shala was writing:

To the councils of revolutionary soldiers and workers – from the representatives of les tribus … the final, the decisive struggle – we are coming to take our place beside you, now that you have shown your readiness to join us. Leave the battlefield, and take up your positions in the streets of the cities – not to fight, but to welcome the revolution which you have accomplished by your refusal to fight …

'We mustn't let this get to the troops who've not yet deserted,' said Shala, as Osman read the leaflet. 'We need as much help as we can – but we can't very well thank "the councils of irresolute soldiers and workers …'

'I suppose, then, we must make contact across the lines here with the troops,' said Osman.

The black dust tasted bitter, Shala thought. 'We need something on the peasants … something for the officers, some statement on the penal commission …' With a touch of annoyance, she remembered Curzon. 'Perhaps we can give him some work on one of the commissions – perhaps transport? But his standing is not high, and he has no interest in administration … Perhaps he can go with Sadik to talk to the troops?'

Curzon and Sadik were told to cross the lines and talk to the government troops. 'Perhaps now,' thought Curzon, 'away from Shala, I can start to think again of the points I've lost sight of … "here there is an incompleteness in the manuscript", so to speak.'

They walked forward.

'I seem to have lost touch with personal motives,' thought Curzon as they struggled through the racking sunlight. 'Not only my own, which are obviously subsumed, swept away, in this hum of events – but Shala's, Osman's. We are being tested for adaptability, and the more adaptable we are, the further we move apart on the current. I can only just discern the outline of forces dwarfing us – so that I can't investigate personal contributions without some kind of microscope. Certainly I lack the equipment needed to analyse any of this.'

He felt, indeed, as he stumbled forward, the weight of past self-indulgence, all the sweeteners, the self-denying intellectual sawbucks he has slipped himself in the past … Able to come to terms with events and their characters only in his head, it was his mind which had suffered most from its diet of necessary but rotten compromise …

Caught out by his style at every turn, he could no longer follow his own ingenuity, let alone Shala's development. Yet how unabsorbing were these reflections … even the interest in himself which had for so many years sustained him seemed now tedious – irrelevant to its author and only reader. His only justifications had been the cultivation of his own sensibility, and this was not only absurd, it no longer even existed – it had been whittled away in the desert.

'No pretension now,' he thought, 'or only pretension.'

'I think we'll push round to the right,' said Sadik. 'We seem to be heading for a part of the line which is still controlled by the officers.'

Curzon peeped at a few words towards the end of the Russian girl's diary – he had taken the manuscript with him to serve, in case of negotiations, as a mock brief.

Could I get to the south – could I get to Sukhum where it is spring? Could I break open the doors of the coachhouse, and harness the horses, and drive them to Sukhum? Or are the traces too heavy, the lock too secure? How would I live in Sukhum away from the poplars, away from the white garden furniture, the lilac trees now as black as charcoal, but with months of summer heat hoarded …

The manuscript burst open, and as the leaves slid across the desert Curzon saw the walls of the town they had left weeks before.

It was not long before a group of twenty soldiers had captured Curzon and Sadik.

'I'm very sorry,' said Curzon.

'Don't think of apologising,' said Sadik. 'It's part of a cautionary tale – as I suppose all tales are.'

Sadik thought, 'All in all, this is not a bad time to be caught: it's only a marginal setback. Curzon never concealed the fact that he was the weakest link, and I made the choice which committed us to him. So – it's a good time for the inevitable to happen …'

And when Curzon could think beyond his shame and apprehension, he thought of Shala and of Osman, whose lives seemed to develop independence and greater definition in proportion as his own dwindled and flickered.

On the railway leading to the city, a train was dragging a fresh load of sabotaged goods to the front.

The driver said, with satisfaction, 'They've stopped firing, but they're still nearer …'

The fireman said, 'We must tell them in the city not to blow up the rails: none of this lot can be used – and we might get hurt if they start blowing us up …'

'Well, we'll soon be finished with the whole business,' said the driver. He thought of the cheese he would be able to make in the autumn, of the ducks sailing into the range of his gun as he hid half under the salty marshes …

A young soldier, one of those taking Sadik and Curzon to the city prison, said, 'You're lucky not to be interrogated … Don't you agree, that revolutionary discipline must be subject to revolutionary morality – and that is sufficient defence of terror?'

'I'm not very interested,' said Sadik. 'That question is not my concern. If I am to be the object of someone's terror, the precise arguments don't make much difference – except perhaps to whether it's to be quick or slow.'

The soldier laughed. 'It's quick, all right. As for me – before I commit myself, I'll wait and see which way the cat jumps … Emancipation! We've waited so long, we can wait a bit longer. Besides, the rations are still coming in.'

'Not for long,' said a sergeant. 'The railwaymen bring in loads of junk – sabotaged, rotten, thieved …'

The lorry passed by houses on the city limits: naphtha lamps hung under the vines in the hot twilight. Here and there a grandfather would pick out a few notes on a dutar: a boy with a donkey held up a melon as the lorry passed. 'Good luck,' he shouted, but this might have been a sarcasm.

Curzon could see a kite in the desert, black against the dark blue of the evening sky, a few puffs of flame and white smoke breaking the outline. Shala was sending a last inscrutable message? Or was this further to the rear than Shala and the political committee had been – no more than a signal from cousin to cousin?

A smell of carnations came to them: 'All the way from the sea,' said Sadik.

A man selling ice-cream was pushing his cart home. He was wearing a tall skin hat, like a Kazak's but he did not look like a Kazak.

'This is where your politics gets you,' said the sergeant. 'Better let things be – if there's change, then let there be change. We've nothing against you. I've a lot against the lords, myself. But I've twenty goats – I'm going to wait a bit now, don't you see? Now, for myself, I think you're right, to do what you did. We're a rare lot of bandits ourselves, in our village … But you're nothing to me. I can get by, with the help of the others, in the regiment, or the village, or the family … Still, you were silly to get caught like that …'

In the guardroom, the firing squad looked forward to their breakfast. The more victims, the more food – though there were signs that as the number of executions increased, the authorities were beginning to tire of maintaining the ritual. There was even talk of dispensing with firing squads altogether, but the men who waited outside the prison walls calculating the weight of the volleys and taking news of the members executed to the partisans, were held to affect morale.

'Ah well, better men than you have been executed,' Curzon was comforted.

'I suppose I should say there are plenty to carry on the work, that we shall win in the end, that I give my life gladly for the peasants and the proletariat. And I suppose it's true. I'm a bit irritated at having tried to understand my environment in order to control it, and then finding I'd made the mistake to land me here. It was a decent mistake to make. I'm sorry that the ones who win won't have made a similar gesture, and I don't think they should. But as you say, not only have better men than me been executed, better men than me are still in the movement, and I've not made their task harder.'

It was still an hour before dawn when they were taken outside.

Written in 1968

about the author

John Fraser has lived in Rome since 1980. Previously, he worked in England and Canada.

www.ingramcontent.com/pod-product-compliance
Lightning Source LLC
Chambersburg PA
CBHW020551310726
48979CB00008B/1166/J

9780956140913